ELLE HARTFORD

A Tale of Rowan and Daisy

Phoenix & Kelpie

First published by Phoenix & Kelpie Press 2023

Copyright © 2023 by Elle Hartford

This novel is entirely a work of fiction. The names, characters and incidents portrayed in it are the work of the author's imagination. Any resemblance to actual persons, living or dead, events or localities is entirely coincidental.

First edition

ISBN: 979-8-9872017-9-4

This book was professionally typeset on Reedsy.
Find out more at reedsy.com

To everyone who read Cold as Snow and loved it . . .

here's something a little bit different,

a little bit romantic,

and very fun!

Contents

A Preliminary Note

From Sir Rowan

I am not, of course, a poet, nor do I aspire to follow in the footsteps of storytellers of old. Usually, I satisfy myself merely with quoting their work. However, my employer, the lady alchemist known as Red, has suggested that I collect my notes regarding this tale, and I have always found it prudent to follow the advice of my employers.

She also informed me that the tale does *not* begin where I thought it would—namely, high on a mountain, in an old snow-blown stone keep, where I first saw my love and nearly fell off my horse. Apparently I am required to give more background leading up to that inciting moment.

I suppose it *would* be difficult to explain the other knights without backstory. Not that they matter very much. But now Miss Red is frowning at me.

Well, a knight strives always to rise to the occasion. Enclosed here is a complete reproduction of my notes from my investigation into the Tree of Life, following the affair which has come to be known as *Cold as Snow.* I have included entries from my daily journal interspersed with other important accounts, which no doubt will become clear as the story unfolds.

As many more wise than I have said, *Once upon a time . . .*

One

A Tale of Pixies

From Sir Rowan's Notes
  Dated the 14th Day of the 1st Moon

Once upon a time there was a queen whose name was Silver-tree, and her daughter, whose name was Gold-tree. One day, Gold-tree and Silver-tree went to a glen, where there was a well, and in the well there was a trout.

Said Silver-tree, "Troutie, am not I the most beautiful queen in the world?"

"Oh indeed you are not," said the trout.

"Who is?" asked Silver-tree, frowning.

"Why, Gold-tree, your daughter."

Silver-tree went home, blind with rage. She lay down on the bed, and vowed she would never be well until she could get the heart and the liver of Gold-tree, her daughter, to eat.

1

At nightfall the king came home, and heard that Silver-tree, his wife, was very ill. He went where she was, and asked her what was wrong with her.

"Oh! only a thing which you may heal if you like," said she.

"Oh! indeed there is nothing at all which I could do for you that I would not do," he promised.

The queen said slyly, "If I get the heart and the liver of Gold-tree, my daughter, to eat, I shall be well."

Now it happened about this time that Gold-tree had made friends with a hermit who lived in a cave, and often talked of going to live with them. The King now agreed to this, and they went away. The king then gave a goat's heart and its liver to his wife to eat; and she rose well and healthy.

A year after this Silver-tree went to the glen, where there was the well in which there was the trout.

"Troutie," said she, " am not I the most beautiful queen in the world?"

"Oh! indeed you are not," answered the trout.

"Who else could it be?" asked the queen.

"Why, Gold-tree, your daughter."

"Oh," laughed the queen, "well, it is long since she was living. It is a year since I ate her heart and liver."

"Oh," replied the trout, "indeed she is not dead. She is living with a hermit in a cave."

Silver-tree went home, and begged the king to gather a hunting party, and said, "I am going to see my dear Gold-tree, for it is so long since I saw her." The party was arranged, and they went away.

It was Silver-tree herself that was at the head of the party, and she led them straight up the mountain in search of the cave.

Meanwhile Gold-tree, who was out gathering flowers, heard the sounds of the queen and party coming. She ran back at once to the

2

cave.

"Oh!" said she to the hermit, "my mother is coming, and she will kill me."

"She shall not kill you at all," said the hermit. "We will lock you in a room where she cannot get near you."

This is how it was done; and when Silver-tree found the cave at last, she began to cry out: "Come to meet your own mother, when she comes to see you." But Gold-tree said that she could not, that she was locked in the room, and that she could not get out of it.

"Will you not put out," said Silver-tree, "your little finger through the keyhole, so that your own mother may give a kiss to it?"

Gold-tree put out her little finger, and Silver-tree went and put a poisoned stab in it, and Gold-tree fell dead.

When the hermit came home, and found Gold-tree dead, they were in great sorrow, and they did not bury her at all, but instead locked her in that room where nobody would get near her.

In the course of time the hermit made friends with a priestess, and gave the priestess the run of the whole cave, except that one room. But one day the hermit forgot to take the key when out on a walk, and the priestess got into the room. What did she see there but Gold-tree, who seemed asleep.

The priestess began to turn and try to wake her, and she noticed the poisoned stab in her finger. She took the stab out, and Gold-tree rose alive, as joyful as ever.

When the hermit came home and saw Gold-tree alive they rejoiced. Said the priestess, "I have done my good work for you, and now I will go away."

"Oh! indeed you shall not go away, but we shall all stay together," said Gold-tree. "And we must hide ourselves away and stay safe, lest Silver-tree come and try to hurt us again."

"She will come again," said the priestess with confidence. "That is

3

the way these tales work."

"She can not hurt us if she can not find us," said the hermit. "Let us think of a plan."

And so the three friends put their heads together. Each of the three came up with a good idea. Gold-tree knew of a way to make a cave so cheerful and bright that they'd never need to leave. The hermit knew of a way to make the cave impossible to find. And the priestess knew how to create a guardian who would keep them safe. With these three assurances, they could live happily and well.

I have copied this story out of a scroll hidden away in Belville's bookstore. It lists its author as a pixie, but none of the pixies who live near Belville could have written it; in fact, Belville's scholar insists that the pixies will have nothing whatsoever to do with this story. A strange prejudice on their part, for pixies are known to love stories.

After the discovery of an enchanted ore at the mine, it seems likely to me that the cave in this story is real. Moreover, I believe it houses the Tree of Life—Gold-tree's contribution, perhaps, to the trio's safety.

That is not to say that I believe any such person as Gold-tree exists. The characters in the story are most likely made up in order to explain a natural phenomenon—namely, the living Tree deep in the mountain, and also its guardian—a dragon. I have seen the dragon only twice. Though Lark, owner of the mine, insists that she has spoken to the dragon, she will tell me nothing about the encounter. My own efforts to meet with the dragon have come to nothing. Therefore, I remain focused on my original goal: to find the Tree of Life.

After all, to find the Tree would not only solve a great mystery, it would atone for the great wrongs I have done.

As the water fairies of Grendale say, *The Tree of Life stems from the root of redemption.*

But the task is a massive one, and there is much ground on the mountain to search. To that end, I express-mailed a request for assistance with the Knight's Court this afternoon. I had my misgivings about it—I doubt my standing with the Court is any good, after my numerous failures, and if I am honest, I thought to myself as I sent out the letter that perhaps I am growing too old for their codes and their bonds. But, nonetheless, I received an approval shortly after my letter sent, and that is something of a relief—I had almost feared they might seek to punish me instead, for venturing out on my own duty.

Since I got approval, I have sent a missive to Sir Lancelot specifically asking for assistance. I doubt any others would be as eager to help a lone knight; Lancelot is always looking for an extra chance at glory. Loth though I am to play host to him and his court of ale-drinking knights, I have a feeling that in order to truly search the mountain, I will need more bodies. Lancelot and his associates must at least be able to identify a cavern or a glowing tree if they find one.

Not to mention a thirty-foot long, monstrous dragon.

Two

Further Introductions

From Daisy's Recollections

Nice to meet you. I'm Daisy.

I don't write many things down. I actually don't write anything down. It's a—family trait, you might say? More of a precaution, really.

So, if I make mistakes, just bear with me. I'm not exactly sure of—well, a lot of things, really. A lot has happened. But that's why I like Red's idea of writing things down.

I thought I ought to start by showing you what my daily life *used* to be like. There were the pixies to take care of—that's what's always at the forefront of my mind, the pixies. It's my job, and we take that kind of thing very seriously in my family. In fact I actually inherited this job from my mother, and she got it from her uncle, and he from his grandfathers before him. But the thing is, I care about them a lot, too. I think it's hard *not* to care about such cute little things. They're like dandelion seeds floating on the wind, but much more colorful.

I don't mean that they *look* like seeds though. They look the way most people picture fairies. Little elven creatures, with glittery wings. Most of them are only six inches tall. They live altogether, at least *my* pixies do, in a bunch of little nests in the Tree.

Oh—maybe that's what I should have started with. The Tree.

But you'll find out plenty about that later, I think. It really did start with the pixies anyway. You see, winter is awfully hard on them, especially since the mining started on the mountain. The wind whistles through the tunnels the miners carve, and even the ground far beneath the snow is cold. And while it's true that pixies are magic and they have the power to keep their home warm and safe, it's also true that pixies are—maybe just a *little* dramatic. I've learned you just have to go with it. And the poor things were working very hard this past winter, trying to keep their nests bright and cozy amid all the storms. So I felt bad for them and I promised to buy them the finest wool from the town down the mountain, so that they could make little tiny scarves for themselves.

It's not really part of my job, I admit. But I just couldn't say no to the thought of all those little pixies smiling in their tiny scarves.

And anyway, it wasn't supposed to be a big deal. I knew one of the residents of the town, and I'd done work for her before. Every once in a while, I find it's handy to have some extra money and to trade for a few luxuries. So I thought this would be like any other time, and that I would work for a weekend, get the yarn, and then be free to go back to my gardening. Maybe, I thought, if I got enough extra yarn, the pixies might make me a shawl too. But that really was all I thought about it.

Three

A Knight's Quest

Sir Rowan
  16th Day of the 1st Moon

I received word from Sir Lancelot this morning; as I suspected, he's bringing several others with him. No doubt they are eager for a chance to deplete someone else's cellars. I recognized one of the names he mentioned, but the others are new to me. I can only hope they are as useful as they will be boisterous.

During lunch I left Red's Alchemy and Potions to inquire with Madame Lavender about the possibility—not to mention the dangers—of hosting such knights. Fortunately, she seemed well acquainted with such situations. A keen businesswoman, Mme Lavender; I have no doubt she's been in Belville much longer than most people think. She's certainly been around long enough to have acquired properties beyond her esteemed tavern on Market Square. In one of these, she has promised, we will be very comfortable. I need only to finish my lists of requirements. She has offered to help procure mead, which is a blessing. And of course, I shall have to notify Miss Red of my absence. It is a pity to have to request leave so soon after beginning my work there, but I feel I must see this through. Above all else, this is why I have stayed in Belville, is it not? And to wait any longer would only be to delay the inevitable.

There is much yet to do before they arrive.

Four

Necessity

Daisy

It might also help to know what I actually did, mightn't it?

You see, the pixies and I lived quite remotely on the mountain, which most people in town never bothered to climb. I think vaguely I remember some rumors about it being haunted, or some such thing. Maybe those came from the old stone tower.

But the tower isn't haunted at all. It's just very old. I'm not sure who built it or why they chose to build it on a mountaintop where there are very bad storms in the winter. Still, they did a good job, because it's still standing.

Lavender says that's because my plants are keeping it up. But that's just a funny joke of hers.

She really is a wonderful person to work for. I don't remember when we met—maybe it was decades ago, or even centuries. I'm fairly certain she's been around as long as the town has, but then I never did think very much of the town at the beginning. Anyway, I met her one day when I was out trying to find a certain mushroom for an ill pixie, and she—Lavender, I mean, not the pixie—started asking all sorts of questions. I was very uncomfortable. But she saw that and just laughed and told me she was only interested because she'd just bought this old stone keep, and she wondered if I'd look after it from time to time? I didn't agree at first. I actually didn't agree until I saw the place. It's just a round stone tower with high walls. But inside the walls are the most *wonderful* gardens.

If my brother ever reads this, he will say it is my weakness—gardening. I guess maybe it is. But I can't stare at pixies *all* day, and neither can I stare at the Tree. So somewhere along the line I picked up a hobby. I think it's a very nice one, myself. Plants are so interesting and soothing to work with.

In any case, that was the arrangement—that I could fix up the gardens there, and keep an eye on the place. And if some people came to stay there I would look after them too. Lavender always paid me very well for doing that. All I had to do was greet them, help them settle in, and check on them each day. I'm not very good at cooking, but sometimes I'd help them get food if I thought they were nice guests. Usually people brought their own supplies, though. You don't go so high up on a mountain without being prepared, after all.

Five

At First Sight

꧁◦◦◦꧂

Sir Rowan
 20th Day of the 1st Moon

As I write this I can hear her moving behind me, sorting dishes.
How is it a decrepit old kitchen such as this can stand to contain
such a person?

But that isn't the beginning. I must collect my thoughts.

Ah, my love's like a red, red rose,
That's newly sprung in snow . . .

I have been remiss in my entries. Though it is my practice
to write at the end of each day, the past few days have been
an unceasing stream of communications from Sir Lancelot.
First he lost the address. Then he wanted to know how much
ale I had on hand. Then he needed reminding of the purpose
behind the visit. Then he wanted to tell me he and his party

were almost here, but they *weren't* almost here, they were nearly halfway up another mountain entirely. Suffice it to say, I am seriously doubting my wisdom in asking them here.

But I'm not doubting my choice to rent out this keep.

Sir Lancelot and his party, numbering four including himself, met me early this morning only slightly after I had intended to make the ascent up the mountain. Nessie was in fine form and we made the trip very quickly, which is a great mercy. We arrived at the keep shortly after tea time, and I was just thinking to myself that perhaps this trip wouldn't be a total waste when the front door of the keep opened and *she* appeared.

I am not sure, upon reflection, if I had actually meant to dismount Nessie so quickly.

I must admit that the one thing of which there is no doubt is that, unfortunately, I do not seem to have made the impression upon our hostess which she made upon me.

Mme Lavender had told me to expect someone by the name of "Daisy," of course, but in the wilds of Belville, such a name could have indicated any number of persons. I did not know if I would be meeting with a fairy, an ogre, or even a giantess. To be quite honest, I don't believe I cared. More fool I!

She came out as we arrived within the outer wall, as I have said. The sun shone upon the highlights in her red hair, and the freckles upon her pale cheeks. I admit these are qualities I have not heretofore admired, but they were mitigated somewhat by her choices of sturdy boots and cloak, and the careful welcome in her eye. I can not say exactly what it was; her proud posture as she approached, perhaps, or the unexpected softness in her voice; or then again, it may have been something as simple as the way her fingertips arched in greeting—arched, that is, before she saw the need to hurry and claim my mount's reins for me.

Well, there wasn't any *real* need for that, of course. Nessie was as cool and calm as ever, though no doubt wondering inwardly what had happened to his master. I did my best to compose myself and to speak to her, but I do not think I succeeded. In fact I remember distinctly that Sir Lancelot was being unconscionably loud:

"We're here! Here we are!" he was saying, or something equally stupid.

"Yes," said she, though she seemed almost alarmed by the fact; her hand upon Nessie's reins trembled. "And you are—?"

"A party of travelers," I said to her, recovering my voice. "I made arrangements with Madame Lavender for use of this keep."

Behind me, like a chorus, went Sir Lancelot and his friends: "Knights! We are knights!"

"Yes," said she again. She looked very carefully at each person in turn, and I could have sworn she saw then right into the depths of my soul. What was it she saw there? The embarrassment of my emotions, the shame of my past, perhaps? Whatever it was, I do not think it worked in my favor.

When she spoke again her voice was strong and clear. "Please, take your things inside and make yourself comfortable in the main hall, and I will see to your mounts."

The others hastened to do as she asked. They all ride the warhorses and chargers which are so common amongst young knights—and which, no doubt, were glad of a rest. But Nessie is no common beast, and I knew he would give her trouble, so I lingered and said I would handle him myself if she would only show me the way.

She did so, rather coolly I thought, but her aspect with the

15

horses was gentle. They gave her no trouble. Nessie however saw fit to bite my shoulder, because I was not paying proper attention whilst removing his saddle. Fortunately, I do not think she noticed.

Six

Knights of Uncertainty

Daisy

Knights. They were KNIGHTS! Lavender didn't warn me they were KNIGHTS.

Of course, she had no idea she might need to. I never told her who I am, only that I like gardening and didn't mind looking after her tower. So it really isn't her fault. She didn't know any different.

Knights.

Seeing them had been a shock like I hadn't had in centuries. From the moment I saw the first one, in his blue cloak and sparkly mail, I might as well have blacked out. He did have a nice horse, though—I did notice that. A water horse, if I'm not mistaken. I've never met one in person, but I've heard of the way they're born from waves and take form by magic.

Would that the horse had come and left the knight behind, I thought.

It had been years upon years since I'd dealt with a knight. But I remember them very vividly from my youth. They were the specters of our nightmares. To this day, my brother is on a crusade against them.

Anyway, it wasn't until I'd unsaddled the last horse that my hands finally stopped shaking. I told myself that obviously the knights didn't recognize me, and had no idea who I was, so therefore I had no reason to be afraid. I just had to be very careful, that's all. I couldn't let even a single thing slip.

Then I got a prickly feeling up my spine and I turned around and the water horse knight was staring at me.

"Forgive me," he said, as though he was going to say something else—but then he didn't. He just looked at me, and I stared at him rather stupidly, wondering what I needed to forgive him for. For being a knight? For something he was about to do? I rocked uneasily from foot to foot, wishing for wings.

Then he lifted the saddle in his arms. "I was not sure where you wished me to put this," he explained.

That's alright, then, I told myself. I took a deep breath and I showed him the tack room. It's very little—the whole stable is small and narrow, and curved, built along the outer wall. So I opened the door and tried to show him, and he tried to go into the room past me, and like a nestling I was so busy watching him that I forgot I should have also been avoiding him, and we ended up stuck together in the doorframe.

I have never, ever been so close to a knight. I only really get that close to pixies. Or plants.

But he didn't seem as dangerous as he should have. Actually he let the saddle slip and he put a hand on my arm, as if he was trying to say he was sorry.

Sometimes I get these insights. Red tells me that most humans don't get them. I don't think anyone in my family does, either, except the ones of us who have lived with the pixies for a long time. It's a side effect of all the magic, I think. It's not like a sixth sense or anything, just a sort of flash—at least, that's what it is for me. There was a moment when he touched me where I could feel warmth, and light, and I could have sworn I heard the pixies laughing, but not cruelly as they sometimes do. It was a joyful feeling—pure joy. It made me dizzy.

But of course, all this poor man knew was that I had stood in his way and then looked like I was about to fall over as soon as he knocked into me accidentally. Looking back, I can see it is a bit funny.

"Please forgive me," he said again, and he kept going, "how very clumsy of me, I'm so sorry to have disturbed you, my lady, I'll be absolutely mortified if I hurt you—"

Meanwhile I was seeing stars. When I finally got hold of myself again, I had a hard time convincing him that I was alright. He kept wanting me to sit down. I wasn't about to let my guard down any further around a knight, but I did smile at him, which seemed to convince him to be quiet.

"It's alright," I told him. "Just a passing spell. Please, don't worry about me."

He sort of ducked over his saddle, which he had dropped on to the ground by then. It took me a moment to realize that he was bowing to me. And—had he called me a "lady"?

Oh dear, I thought. I had wanted to deceive him about myself, but I hadn't meant to pretend I was somehow royal.

"It's quite alright," I repeated, not sure what else to say. "Here,

I'll help you put away your things, and then I'll show you the way to your companions. They must be wondering about us by now."

He bowed again, and as we picked up his tack, he asked, "Did you provide mead in the main hall?"

"Of course," I said. "It serves as the dining hall as well, and there is always a tap there. And a fire, too."

"In that case, my lady, I do not think we need concern ourselves with them. I doubt very much they are worried," he said.

I looked up at him then, really looked at him. He was very tall for a human—I know this because I myself am tall, but my eyes only came up to his nose. It was the humor in his voice as he spoke that made me look. It was a very dry sound, like a dam holding back an ocean of observations behind his words. It made me laugh even though I knew nothing of the other knights.

He had a stone face—that is how I think of people like him. The kind of face that is very smooth and impassive normally. But his eyes were very blue and his hair very dark, and so when his eyebrows lifted in surprise, the effect was unmistakable. It was like he was someone else entirely. This made me want to laugh again, and so I turned away and hid my smile, because I didn't want him to think I was laughing at him out of a mean spirit.

As I ducked ahead of him into the tack room and folded the saddle blanket and put it away, he moved quietly. But then after a moment, when I was done and had turned toward the door—and him, he said, "It has occurred to me that I should have introduced myself."

"I know who you are," I told him, and I smiled because my

voice sounded quite light, even though inside I was buzzing with nerves. "Lavender told me it was someone named Rowan who made the arrangements, and I think that must be you."

"True," he said, and he bowed again, this time very low. I began to wonder if he ever got tired of doing that. "And you are the caretaker of this keep, are you not, my lady?"

"I'm Daisy," I told him, feeling a bit shy about all this respect. You always hear about knights being respectful, of course, but I'd never experienced it. To be honest, I'd always thought it must be exaggeration, or wishful thinking. "You can just call me Daisy. I'm not really in charge of this place, or anything like that."

"It is an honor to meet you nonetheless," he said, and I got the idea he meant it very sincerely. This made me blush even more, not least because I wasn't at all sure that *I* found it an honor to meet a knight. But I could hardly say so.

I suppose I said something, though, and we did manage to make it out of the tack room without bumping into each other again. We crossed the yard quickly—I was focused on my winter flowers, which were perking up nicely in the sunshine. The moment I let him in through the front door of the tower, we could hear his companions in the main hall:

What shall we do with a drunken squire?
What shall we do with a drunken squire
What shall we do with a drunken squire
Earl-ye in the mor-ning!

The front door of the keep lets into a hallway which branches off to both the left and the right, and on both sides it becomes a stairwell which circles the tower up all four stories. Inside that ring of staircases, the inner rooms of the tower are very snug, especially when the fire is going. There are windows lined up with openings on the stairs so that some lights get in, but usually you have to use candles and torches to get around. Some guests have used magic lights, too, but it seems like such a waste when you could use perfectly good firelight.

In any case, the other knights had made themselves quite at home. I could see that Sir Rowan didn't approve exactly, but I thought it was a good thing because it meant they wouldn't be worrying about me. Maybe he thought that they should be worried? I wondered. I started to get a little more wary of him again, and I went off to the kitchen as soon as I'd told them how to get to their rooms on the second and third floors.

The kitchen is my favorite room in the keep. It's beneath the main hall, so I guess it's technically the basement, but it doesn't feel gloomy or dirty. There's only one staircase down, so on the opposite wall there's real windows to the outside, set down into the ground. I thought the window wells were the perfect place for perennial herbs and other plants which need more shelter from the winter. Between the windows and the hearth, there's a lovely yellow, green, and orange light. Maybe living with the pixies so long has made me especially appreciative of color. In any case, the kitchen is my own little stronghold, and I like it there. I was feeling quite secure again until the knights came crashing down the stairs at dinner time.

Seven

Dinner and a Show

Sir Rowan
  20th Day of 1st Moon, cont

Nessie was right to bite me. I have let my concentration slip abominably.

And yet I can't help thinking that, had the others not been present, the evening would have been quite pleasant. Although I must admit it was quite a shock coming down the stairs. The kitchen is in the cellar, and naturally it is warmer there than in the rest of the keep; still, without the use of magic enhancements, it could hardly be considered cozy. And yet my lady had shed her cloak and revealed herself to be wearing pink overalls and a white linen shirt, the hems all rolled up. She did look very much a gardener, I will admit to that. She also looked even more becoming than she had before.

Sir Lancelot and his cronies beat me to speaking.

"Dinner! Dinner!" chorused the knightlings, one of whom I am vaguely familiar with—a pale tower of a man, half giant, who goes by the moniker "the Black Knight"—and the other of whom I have never before encountered, a dark-skinned lionkin lass who seems to prefer the name "Salna." Sir Percveal had, rather wisely, decided to wait in the great hall.

Sir Lancelot, meanwhile, had apparently noticed that his hostess was female and presumably of marriageable age. He immediately began showering her with all sorts of overblown compliments which I can not bring myself to repeat.

I couldn't help but notice that Daisy seemed disturbed by this onslaught. I might have taken some satisfaction in the others' failure, I admit. However to see her pressed back against the sink, her hands lifted as if to cover her white face, was unbearable. I stepped forward at once and scattered the ill-mannered charlatans with the announcement that *I* would be the one to make dinner, and I required them to procure some of the provisions left in the stable with the horses. A look of concern crossed Daisy's face as the trio clamored up the stairs on their task.

"Perhaps," said she, very quietly and uncertainly, "I should have offered to show them where to go."

"Absolutely not," said I, thinking of her stuck in that stifling tack room surrounded by knightlings. "My lady, you have already done quite enough; do not let them badger you into thinking you must do more."

"But it's bound to take them a while to find what you asked for," she pointed out.

"I should certainly hope so," I said, as I set aside my cloak and rolled up my sleeves. "But that need not delay our dinner."

"But . . ." Her gentle voice trailed off, and she shifted so that she leant against the counter, watching me as I arranged the provisions I'd brought down earlier. When I risked a glance back at her, I saw she had begun to smile. "I see. You wanted them to leave."

"I find that cooking is best done without a raucous audience. I hope you do not think me rude for having sent them off?"

"No," she said, and there was a laugh in her voice now. "No, actually I was thinking, that might be a good idea for dealing with the pixies, too."

"The pixies?" I paused. If she had dealt with them, I thought, perhaps she could be even more valuable to my search than the knightlings. "You deal with them often, then? I would not have thought them to come up so high on the mountain."

"Oh—they don't," she said. Her face had gone pale again, and she turned abruptly to tend some of the plants which overflow the kitchen windows. "It was—a slip. Just a silly thing to say, really."

I let the matter end there, because I did not like to see her uncomfortable, or even yet to think that *I* had made her uncomfortable somehow. In the silence I resumed making dinner, a stew which I felt would be a welcome refreshment after a day of riding. Though I had brought the ingredients with me—Mme Lavender having apprised me of the situation in the keep—I had not brought the necessary equipment. As I moved through the kitchen, finding a soup pot and the utensils I needed, I found it very gratifying that Daisy stayed nearby. She tended to her potted plants with admirable focus. But after some time had passed, and the silence had grown comfortable, I became aware that she was watching me once more.

"I hope you don't mind," she said, blushing when I looked up over the table. "I . . . I'm not a very good cook, myself. I always like it when the guests know what they're doing. It's . . . it's soothing to watch."

"It is very soothing to work in such a well-appointed kitchen," I returned, acknowledging her kindness.

She smiled. She was leaning on the counter again, her hands wrapped loosely around her waist. Though she stood across the room from the fire, she didn't seem cold. "Lavender let me set it up however I wanted," she told me, "and I tried to do it so that it makes sense, even though I don't do much cooking myself."

"It is imminently sensible," I assured her. After a moment, I gathered the courage to add, "Would you perhaps like to practice your skills?"

"You mean, help you cook?" She cocked her head, her eyes alight, and for a moment I wondered if she might be fae.

"If you would like to," I managed.

It took her a moment, but she smiled again at me, and stepped forward. "I'd like that, yes. And if you want, you could use some of the herbs from the pots. I could go out into the garden—"

"Please, my lady," I interrupted. It was rude, yes, but I didn't want her venturing into the cold on my account. "There won't be any need for that. I shall be quite content with what you have collected here, I am sure."

She proved to be a very capable sous-chef, and very adept at handling the roots and vegetables. At some point, she admitted to me that her great failing as a cook lay in choosing seasonings, rather than in the preparation. Indeed as she chopped squash for the stew she seemed almost relaxed, and I was very glad to see it; and once, I had the opportunity to brush her hand as we traded knives, and in that moment I knew that we could season

26

the stew with bushels of fiery peppers for all I cared—it would still be the greatest meal I'd ever had. She looked at me with such a careful eye when I touched her, but when I apologized, she smiled.

Eight

Bitter Rumors

Daisy

I never really thought that cooking might be fun. Maybe that's why I've never been good at it. But when it was just me and Sir Rowan in the kitchen, and he was talking very kindly the way he does, and a little stiffly and amusingly too, I thought I could see how cooking might be a very fun, very comfortable thing.

Except for the fact that he was a knight.

It was fast becoming apparent to me, though, that there were differences between knights. I must admit I always used to think of them as all the same. They are all basically the same in stories, which I think is the bad thing about manners, perhaps—with all of them running around saying "sire" this and "if you please" that, and bowing to ladies and slaying everything in sight, how could anyone tell them apart? But Sir Rowan wasn't at all like his companions. And what's more, *he* didn't seem to think of himself as one of them, either.

I think I really realized this when dinner was ready. He'd gone up to the main floor—he said he wanted to tell them, but I wondered if perhaps he didn't want them to come down again. I stood there by the door to the stairs, turning this over in my mind. It was a little strange to me. I guess I stood there a long time thinking about it, because I hardly noticed his footsteps coming back down the stairs, and when he opened the door it actually collided with my shoulder blade.

Naturally he apologized, and profusely, too. He'd caught me with his arm around my other shoulder, stopping me from pitching forward. I stood there tucked under his arm not really listening to his words—I was busy thinking again, this time about how odd it was that I should think it natural for him to apologize, even though he was a knight and therefore very violent by nature; and then again, how strange to think a violent man would be so nice to his horse or so good at making stews.

His hold on me tightened. "My lady?"

I still thought it strange to respond to such a title, but he sounded so affected I had to take pity on him. "It was my fault for standing so near the door," I told him. "Normally I'm not so absent-minded. But it has been . . . a very strange day."

"I do hope you have not found us to be trying guests," he said, his brow creased as he peered down at me.

I smiled at him because they *were* awfully trying, but at the same time, it was so clear how hard he was trying *not* to be so. "Sir Rowan, you shouldn't worry about me."

"That, my lady, is a very tactful answer." But he returned my smile, and he hesitated before stepping away. I wasn't just standing still, I realized—I was leaning into him. Through his apron and his fine silk clothing, his body felt cold. *Maybe I am trying to warm him,* I thought, confused.

"However," he added, "if you insist we are not trouble, perhaps you would like to eat with us?"

"Oh," said I, startled but not quite enough to lean away from him. "No, that's alright. It's nice of you to offer, but I think I will eat here in the kitchen."

"As you wish," he said, "but please, tell me that you will eat some of the stew you helped prepare, and not some tired provisions you have stowed away."

This made me think of a squirrel, and I chuckled. "I promise," I told him.

The words were so new. I never had to promise anyone anything. The pixies knew full well that I would do my duty, and Lavender was always too forgiving to extract a promise.

Sir Rowan let me go then, and I helped him prepare the food to take upstairs. After he was gone, I perched upon the kitchen table with my fragrant meal. It smelled much better than anything I'd ever made—or helped make—before.

But I was a little anxious, so as soon as I'd eaten, I closed the door very carefully and I checked on the pixies. Whenever I leave them, they make sure to charm a new trinket for me to use so that I can look in on them. The charm wears off after a time, I suppose, or sometimes I just lose them once I get back home—I'm not used to having a lot of *things.* This time it was a little locket they'd given me to wear on a chain. I opened it up and let the magic flow through me, and soon I could see they were quite alright.

More than alright, in fact. They were dancing their little dances all around the Tree, and making plans for the scarves they'd make.

This made me smile. Emboldened, I decided that I would go up and check on Sir Rowan too, and see if I might clear some dishes away from the main hall.

I raced up the stairs, quick and very quiet—not on purpose, but only because it is my habit to move quietly if I can, otherwise sometimes the pixies complain at me. The kitchen staircase opens at the back of the main hall, near the great fireplace. The knights had closed the door to keep the heat in, which was fine. But I hesitated a little before I opened it.

"And that's my new quest," I heard one of them—the one who leaned over me in the kitchen—Sir Lancelot, I think—saying. Aside from Sir Rowan he was the most memorable of the knights, because he talked like everyone ought to be listening. "No doubt the poor thing's imprisoned in some tower nearby. Could even be this one—what a coincidence that'd be, eh, Rowan? How much do you know of the cleaning lady?"

Me? Did he mean me? I drew back.

"Daisy is caretaker of this place," said Sir Rowan, rather curtly. "There is no 'cleaning lady.' And she is not imprisoned. She is employed by a very honorable innkeep in town."

"Not a princess in disguise, then?" asked another of the knights. They sounded awfully disappointed.

I thought about this. I hated to burst in on them just as they were talking about princesses—it was hard enough that Sir Rowan thought me a 'lady.' *Although,* I realized, *he clearly knows my situation. So he must not mean it literally.*

"Well, nevermind my quest for a moment, then," Sir Lancelot spoke again. "Don't you think it's time you told us why you've brought us all the way up here into this godsforsaken winter, Rowan?"

"As I explained in my letter," began Sir Rowan, and I admit

I leant in to listen, because I was very curious (and I never said I was as well-mannered as knights are supposed to be), "it has come to my attention that the Tree of Life is hidden somewhere in this area. Not a moon ago, the miners discovered ore touched by its influence. It is my intention to find it, but I can not search the entire mountain alone."

"Tree of Life," muttered the gruffest and oldest of the knights—Sir Perceval, I think. I can not be sure, because my heart had leapt into my throat and my blood was pounding in my ears. "Come, lad, isn't there an ancient dragon guarding that Tree?"

"An ancient and terrible dragon!"

"That is, if the tree itself is not a myth!"

"It will be an epic fight," said Sir Lancelot, sounding very gratified. "You were right to bring in back up."

"It is not my intention to fight the dragon, if indeed there *is* a dragon," said Sir Rowan. I was so confused and alarmed and yet nearly relieved at hearing all this that it seemed to me I was gasping for breath, and that he must hear me behind the door. But he went on quite naturally, "It seems plausible to me that any guardian of the Tree would only wish to fight those who mean the Tree harm. But I do *not* mean it harm."

"Well then what do you mean?"

Sir Rowan did not answer.

Sir Lancelot scoffed. "Still thinking about past deeds, are you, Rowan?"

Again, Sir Rowan did not answer.

The other knights began to clamor. I thought I might faint, but I remained stubbornly until the end.

"Oh, it's only an old affair," said Sir Lancelot carelessly. "Not a tale worth telling. But I can tell you what he wants. He wants to revive the dead."

"Can the Tree of Life do that?"

It can't, I thought. *At least, I'm fairly certain that it can't . . .*

"The main thing," said Sir Rowan, very quietly, "is to find it. That is all."

"Seems to me," said Sir Perceval, "that, seeing as we're in a forest, the dragon might be easier to find than the tree."

You may say I am not so very brave after all, and I will not argue with you. The truth is that upon hearing that, I turned tail and fled down the stairs.

I wanted to curl up under the table. I wanted, actually, to huddle under a blanket under the table, and to barricade myself in with potted plants. Instead I paced, and paced, and paced.

The Tree, I thought.

To find the Tree meant to find the pixies.

The pixies weren't meant to be found.

This was my duty.

They could *die* if someone from the outside found them.

Even someone as nice as Sir Rowan? I wondered.

But he *isn't* nice, I reminded myself firmly. He's a knight. That is, he *might* be nice, but he is still a knight. No matter what else he is, he is a knight, and he has a duty too and he will do his duty just like you will do yours.

I did not like where these thoughts were going at all.

Nine

A Storm is Coming

Sir Rowan
  21st Day of the 1st Moon

I had thought yesterday full of disruptions and pleasures, but today both have intensified. *Love is the color of the sunset,* as the old bards said. But I really *will* stay on track this time, and write everything down.

The morning dawned cold and gray. I was first up, aside I believe from Daisy; I went to look for her in the kitchen but she was already in the garden, staking winter squashes. Today she wore cutoff overalls with brown leggings underneath, and I noticed she'd left her cape on a nearby bench. Her hair was bound back with a scarf. She was working so industriously that I hated to disturb her, especially since I had no proper reason to: I already knew where to find everything I needed in her homey kitchen.

In retrospect perhaps I *should* have gone to talk to her, for all the good I managed to do in the kitchen while my mind was elsewhere.

However the knightlings were soon up, goaded on no doubt by Sir Perceval. He, at least, recognized the seriousness of the outing, though I admit I was disturbed by his ideas about a dragon guarding the Tree. I had heard the rumors as well, of course. And of course I myself have seen the dragon over Belville, weeks ago. But—I can't quite shake the feeling that this is a different kind of dragon than Sir Perceval expects. There *are* different kinds of dragons; everyone acquainted with *The Encyclopedia Draconicus* ought to know that. And while in my youth I may have come across the red and blue types, this dragon—I repeat it because I still can not quite believe it myself—this dragon above Belville was white, and it flew on glittering wings reminiscent of a dragonfly's. To this day I am not sure what it means, but I *do* know there is no such dragon in the *Encyclopedia.*

Once our party was saddled and venturing into the woods, I tried to pull Sir Perceval aside and explain this. Unfortunately, one of the knightlings rode up very close behind us and overheard me speak. As if his numerous sins needed adding eavesdropping to the list! Well, at once he was determined to catch this new dragon, "for science." He got all the others riled up about it, and Sir Lancelot was very sour at me for "holding back" information.

It's not that I am afraid of encountering the dragon. But gods know I am not fool enough any more to look for a battle unprepared!

This trip has not been at all as I expected it to be.

The knights and I number five, so I split us into three groups, myself alone. I paired Sir Perceval with the idiotic Black Knight, thinking he might at least control the damage. Sir Lancelot, when he is not posturing, seems to get on rather well with Salna, so I was pleased with the arrangement. We were to search the first quadrant of the mountain and yet alway remain within horn's distance of each other, in case one of us *did* encounter the mysterious dragon. We did not, however, get very far.

Lunch time had barely passed when the thunder began. I am loth to admit that with the thick cover of treetops overhead, I hadn't noticed the gathering clouds. Yes, perhaps it is true my mind was preoccupied—not with the dragon but with Daisy; I wanted her to feel comfortable and at ease, and I knew I had not accomplished this, and could not be certain why. In fact the only thing I *did* know for certain was that my own need to see her happy was alarming in its intensity.

But the storm, the storm. I must focus. It came upon us incredibly fast. It reminded me of the storms we would get sometimes at the lake, and I knew well how those could develop in the blink of an eye over the water. It seemed to me that this one was no different. I called to the other knights and insisted we make for the keep at once.

"A moment," Sir Lancelot cried. "Sir Perceval has had a stunning good idea."

I might have known then that something was amiss, for I had found the four of them together, rather than split into two search parties. And Sir Perceval would not look at me.

"We must go back before we can not find our way at all," I said as the snow began to fall thickly through the trees.

"You go on ahead, and we'll follow your tracks," said Sir Lancelot. "We won't be far behind. Get the fires going for us, eh?"

This was utter nonsense, and I knew as much at the time. However I thought that the storm would soon change their minds, even though I could not. So I spurred Nessie back to the keep.

The thunder rolled again as Nessie and I came through the outer gate. It was not like the storms at the lake, where the clouds are so high above the water; this storm felt like it must be riding on my shoulders. As I dismounted, Nessie was stamping and shivering with fright. I took him into the stable at once and promised to come check on him in a moment, but first I knew I needed to find Daisy.

My lady was still in the garden, kneeling over beds of kale and hardy greens. While I appreciated her dedication to our foodstuffs, it was hardly the time to linger out of doors. I called to her as I ran up, light snowflakes swirling around my cloak and boots. Overhead, the thunder broke again.

She looked up at the sound, startled, and an unreadable look passed across her face as she saw me.

"A storm is coming up the mountain," I informed her, rather breathlessly I must admit. "We must make ready."

"Oh! I can't believe I didn't notice." Her gaze slid over my shoulder as she took in the rumbling gray clouds, which were quickly turning the afternoon into twilight. I remember her manner distinctly, because at the time I thought it so strange that it should mirror my own thoughts just moments before. "I need to close up all the windows," she said, "and you should go in by the fire. Are the others there already?"

"They are coming," I said. The snow came faster, obscuring her bright hair. "Please allow me to help you in any way I can."

She hesitated, but agreed. And then she reached out for my

hand and pulled me along with her to the nearest door. It was good she did that, rather than spend more time trying to tell me what to do. Although I couldn't help but regret the fact that I wore gloves, and probably the snow collected on them was chilling her hand; she'd thrown her garden gloves down earlier, while we spoke.

With smooth efficiency she led me into the staircase and showed me how to retrieve the wooden shutters from above the windows and put them into place in the open window wells. It is a great weakness of old keeps like this one, that the windows must be left open all the time for light; and as Daisy and I made our way through the tower, she closing up the outer windows and I closing up the inner ones, a thick gloom fell in our wake. The world outside was utterly silent except for the thunder, which was getting louder and louder. In places, wind began to whistle through the stones of the outer wall.

"There's nothing to be done for that," Daisy told me. "I've tried all kinds of things. Not even magic helps. I think old keeps like this are just meant to be drafty. If the storm goes all night, we'll just have to stay down in the kitchen."

I wasn't sure how I felt about the other knights crowding into her space, but at the time I was too busy to give the matter much thought. We worked our way up one spiral staircase and down the other, until we'd covered the entire tower. As we went, Daisy took care to close and latch all the doors, even allowing me to help her hold them in place when the wind picked up still more and tried to blast them open before she could close the latch.

We were just boarding up the last windows on the ground floor when we noticed the others in the courtyard. It was Daisy who saw them; the snow was already several inches deep on the ground and falling fast enough to pass for fog around the keep, but the plunging of the frightened horses was visible, as was the glint of the knights' armor.

"I have to go help them," she said, making for the front door. I followed close behind, not letting her out of my sight.

It was no work at all for her to convince the knightlings to go inside, rattled as they were. They were glad to hand over their reins to her. Even Sir Perceval handed off his mount to me and passed inside; at the time I made nothing of it, but now I wonder.

I wonder, too, if perhaps Mme Lavender hired Daisy because she is as good with creatures as she is with plants. It seemed that as soon as she touched them, the horses calmed. She led two into the stable, leaving me to follow with the other pair, and at once we both set to work. The stable was very dark, but its place along the wall sheltered it from the worst of the wind, and the thick blanket of hay stored in the rafters muffled the sounds of the thunder. I'd shed my gloves while fiddling with the window latches and now I shed my cloak too, working as fast as I could to unsaddle the horses.

Daisy was still faster, though, being more familiar with the stable and the tack room. As I put away the last of the tack, she was already feeding and soothing the horses in their stalls. When she met me in the stable hall, she smelled of sweet hay and her hair, wet and freed from its scarf, framed her eyes, which were luminous in the dark.

"I think we have done it," she said to me, her voice quiet so as not to scare the horses. She was panting slightly, and smiling too, satisfied. "We ought to take some firewood in with us when we go, but other than that . . ."

Her voice trailed off as she looked at me, her gaze traveling down from my hair—no doubt shockingly disheveled—to my shirtsleeves, soaked through across my shoulders where my cloak had given way to the snow—and last to my gloveless hands, which I had been trying unsuccessfully to dry on the coarse fabric of my vest. I stopped what I was doing at once, letting her take my hands into hers meekly.

"You are so cold," she murmured softly. "Oh, I should never have let you come out here with me." And she took my hands and placed them on either side of her face. Her cheeks were hot, almost unbearably so, and her eyes on mine, full of remorse and tenderness, were irresistible. I nearly kissed her then. But I held myself back, because I did not want to take liberties.

"Think nothing of it," I told her. I think I may be forgiven if my voice was quite hoarse. "There was nothing you could have said that would have kept me from following you."

She was standing so near me, and her eyelashes were wet with melting snow. Somehow we had shifted, and instead of her pressing my fingers into her skin, I was now cupping her face very gently, running my thumb over her cheekbone to remove an icy smudge. My fingertips slid into her hair. Even the edges of her ear were warm.

"You have been very kind." Her gaze dropped from mine, and she shivered, though whether that was from the cold or my touch, I couldn't say. She didn't step back. In fact she was leaning into me, just as she had the night before, and with one hand she toyed with the crest sewn into the breast of my shirt.

"No, my lady," I told her, my voice barely above a whisper. "It has merely been my honor to aid you." *To aid you.* How dearly I wished then, and how dearly I wish now, that I might do more.

As if perhaps she knew this, my lady looked up at me once more, and she smiled. And then, very sweetly, she kissed me.

Ten

Snow and Kisses

Daisy

I know. I know what you are thinking! Heavens forbid my brother ever reads any of this, because I'm certain *he* won't understand.

Why in Beyond should I have kissed that knight—that's what everyone will want to know.

Honestly, it seems obvious to me. Especially since the very first time he touched me, it felt like the whole world was singing. Knowing that, I think the real question is why shouldn't I have kissed him sooner. I mean, aside from the fact that he was a *knight.*

When I kissed him then, the first time, standing there in the shadows in the stable, it was just like that first touch all over again. For the second time I got that impossibly *light* feeling,

41

like I was flying, and the pixies were dancing all around me, and there were rainbows running through my veins. I've never felt any magic so strongly. I don't really have any magic of my own, except what the pixies give me, and I've always suspected that to *them* it must feel like rainbows, but I've never felt anything like that myself.

And I think that annoyed me, just a little. I only kissed him for a moment, and when the feeling ended and I was still standing there on my tiptoes with his breath on my lips, I got annoyed because I had kissed him and I hadn't really felt *him.* So I kissed him again.

That time it went much better. I kissed him more deeply, putting my arms around his neck, and he wrapped his around my waist and held me very close to him, like there was nothing else outside us two. His body was so chilled at first, and I remember that because it pleased me very much to feel him warm up in response to my touch. He felt so solid and he tasted like snow, and I liked the way he pressed into me, leaning over me as if he believed already that I must be his.

And I think it's worth saying that when my common sense returned and I pulled back, he let me go very gently. Only his gaze clung to my face, and his fingers tugged at my waist.

"We ought to go back," I said, trying very hard to make my thoughts make sense, "before the snow drifts are so high that we can't get there at all."

There was a boarded-up window over his shoulder, and I could hear the wind tearing at it. But he didn't bother looking out to see what our chances might be. He just looked at me, until finally he straightened. "Of course, my lady," he said. "You know best. Shall we take wood with us, too?"

I turned and led him over to the firewood shed before letting myself smile. I grinned like a fool with no one but the horses to see me, and inside my chest I shivered with the warmth of it all. That was when I decided that actually, I liked it when he called me "my lady."

Eleven

Power of a Name

～◈～

Sir Rowan
  21st Day of the 1st moon, cont.

I have never been kissed the way my lady kissed me then. Never
have I felt quite so desired, nor so desirous.

And yet she was right to focus on the situation at hand. Had
we been trapped in the stable—well, I doubt it would have been
unpleasant; in fact it could have been much nicer than staying
with the other knights. But it would have been very difficult
not to pursue any further liberties, and the last thing I want
is to press her or place her position with Mme Lavender in
danger.

I followed as she led me to the auxiliary room where the
kindling is kept, determined to be of use, and yet unable to
help noticing that she smiled as she glanced back at me, and the

44

tip of her ear poked through her wet hair. I wanted very much to catch her round the waist and kiss her there, and along her neck and at the dimples in her cheeks.

Instead I held very still as she stacked wood in my arms. She didn't look up at me as she worked, not until the very end. Then she surveyed me and realized I had shed my cloak, and as my hands were full, she insisted upon getting it for me. She arranged it carefully over my shoulders, pinning the catch at my throat, and reaching up she smoothed my hair before pulling the hood over my head. Her fingertips brushed my cheek as she settled the fabric around me, and that was the moment that I knew without a doubt that I was hers.

Her timing was perfect. The full force of the storm had reached us by then. Snow piled up in the yard around the keep, and the wind nearly whipped the stable door off the hinges when she opened it. In one arm she cradled kindling, and with her free hand she held on to the edge of my cloak as we crossed to the keep, as though she was afraid I might blow away or get lost in the snow. Perhaps I could have, if I hadn't been so focused on her. The world a mere arm's length away was obscured in white. The tower itself was only a shadow until we stood upon the front step, stamping at the snow drifts and tugging at the heavy door.

Daisy ushered me inside and turned. I think she meant to insist that I go up to the second floor, where the old bathrooms have been converted into steam rooms. That is what I might have thought too in her place. However, the moment the door closed behind us, we realized this was impossible. The main floor of the keep was dark; the great fire in the hall had gone out. Above our heads, wind howled through the upper floors.

"They must be downstairs already," she said. Her voice was

uneasy, and her free hand went to the chain at her throat. But before I could say anything, she crossed the hall to the kitchen stairs.

Well, of course they *were* there, and having a jolly time drinking mead in front of the one fire they'd managed to keep alive. All four of them clustered around the hearth, having dragged over stools and benches from all over Daisy's kitchen. When they saw us one of the knightlings made a face like he was about to jeer, but the other three glanced between one another and fell silent.

The more I write, the more I wonder if somehow Sir Perceval and the knightlings had some hand in bringing down the storm. While I respect Sir Perceval greatly, he *has* been known to meddle with magic, and meddling with magic rarely goes well.

"There you are," cried Sir Lancelot, recovering himself. "You must be freezing. Come sit, come sit!"

"How can it be that you're not even wearing a cloak?" the Black Knight asked of Daisy.

Daisy, who had been walking beside me, stopped. The kitchen was lit only by the fireplace, but I think she blushed and did not like this attention. Though I knew it was rude, I stepped in front of her to confront the young man.

"There are some who will meet a challenge no matter what state they find themselves in," I told him. "Not every one insists upon donning tailor-made armor before doing what must be done."

This made the other knights guffaw, and I must admit I was glad of the chance to say something. The knightling had taken nearly twice as long as the rest of us to be ready that morning.

Sir Lancelot repeated his welcome, and Daisy cleared her throat. "A moment, first," she said. "Sir Rowan, let me show you where the firewood is kept."

I followed her away from the knights, to a sort of pantry tucked into the wall beneath the stairs. There, she unloaded the wood from my arms into an orderly storage chamber. It seemed to me we would be well stocked through the night, especially as we now had to worry about only one fire. There'd be no chance of lighting a new fire upstairs and getting the knights to remove themselves, I feared.

I wanted to make some comment about this, perhaps to offer to *try*, at least, but her gentle hand on my arm stopped me. "Thank you," she murmured, low enough that only I could hear her, shielded in my shadow as she was. What specifically she meant to thank me for I could not say, but I thrilled to hear her address me so intimately. "I was thinking," she added, "I doubt the steam upstairs will work at all, but it might be a good idea for you to change into dry clothes, at least."

"A prudent thought, my lady," said I, acknowledging her, "but what of yourself?"

"Oh—I have a room, here," she whispered, gesturing discreetly over her shoulder. Looking carefully in the darkness, I could see the outline of a door I had not noticed before just beyond the pantry. "I'll go and change, and then we should—well, that is, someone should—"

I got the sense she was hesitant to take charge of a bunch of wayward knights. I doubt such a thing was in her normal line of work, though I had not seen her hesitate like this before. While I could not blame her, this seemed a little strange, because she had been entirely competent in directing me earlier. I thought then that perhaps the idea of dealing with a small crowd intimidated her—or worse, one of the other knights reminded her of some old unpleasant encounter. Nonetheless she knew what ought to be done, and I was glad to follow her line of thinking.

"I will begin arranging dinner on my return," I told her, "and while you need not feel any pressure to assist, I hope you will partake of a warm meal."

She smiled brightly in the dark, and repeated, "Thank you, Sir Rowan," before vanishing into her room.

I turned to leave also, only pausing a moment to inform the others of my plan. In my room I selected the warmest of my tunics and did what little could be done for my hair, thinking that the one good thing about our situation was that it was dark in the kitchen, and my dishevelment might not be so apparent. I decided upon my return to make a roast, which would certainly keep the other knights happy, and would make good use of the roaring fire. Daisy wasn't there at first when I came back down, but she soon appeared and offered to help with the potatoes. Dressed in leggings and a very finely woven sweater, she looked quite at ease, though the way she stuck to my side made me wonder if that was true.

My suspicions were confirmed when we ate, and she opted to sit on the table behind me, rather than clustered on chairs around the fire with the others. While I was more than happy to provide any buffer she needed, I did worry that not enough of the fire's heat would reach her. I hesitated to bring this up, though, not wanting her to feel singled out.

The window wells around the kitchen had long since filled with snow, and the storm outside may as well have been in another world. After eating, the other knights calmed down, and soon fell into sharing stories—that is, listening to Sir Lancelot's stories, or occasionally Sir Perceval's. I never did ascertain what they had done after I left them in the snow, though I did attempt to probe the knightlings about it. They became very nervous when I brought up the topic, and I concluded that somehow they *had* caused the storm, or amplified it, and now were feeling the guilt.

As well they should! It is an ill-advised soul who tampers with nature. They were lucky, all of us were lucky, that Daisy keeps the tower in good repair, and keeps her head in an emergency.

When at last the others had rolled up in spare blankets and nodded off around the fire, I took one more chance of speaking with her. She'd gone upstairs one last time to check on the keep; after a while, she came back down, and I met her at the stairs. I started to speak as soon as she came in, for I had many things on my mind to say, but she glanced at the others and put a finger over her lips. Then she waved at me to follow her, and she brought me into her room. I couldn't see much of it in the dark aside from the fact that it is a small, well-appointed space; I admit I didn't spare any more thought for it than that, because my attention was wholly on her as she closed the door behind us and leant her back against it.

Even as she did so, she looked up at me with wide eyes, as though she'd just then realized the situation we were in. "Oh," she said softly, "I hope I haven't made you uncomfortable. I only wanted to talk without waking the others."

"You needn't worry, my lady," I told her, and since she had mentioned them, the first thought in my head spilled out. "In fact I had hoped for a chance to make you an offer, that is, you may find this unnecessary, but if you like, I could sleep in front of your door tonight."

She leaned back against the door as she looked up at me, her hair falling down over one shoulder. "Actually, I think I *would* like that," she said earnestly. "I know it may seem a little silly, but—but I would appreciate that very much, Sir Rowan."

"Think nothing of it," I assured her, and before I could say anything else she added in a rush,

"I wanted to apologize for—for earlier."

"Apologize? Why?" I wanted to know.

"Because—I just thought—maybe I had . . . pushed you, a little bit," she said, looking down, "because you are so proper."

I saw what she meant and I wanted to laugh, because I myself had had similar worries. "My lady, did I seem unwilling?"

"No," she whispered at last, looking back up.

"Because nothing could be farther from the truth," I assured her, and took my chance to ask, "May I ask for a favor?"

"Of—of course," she said, a little uncertainly. I came nearer to her, just a step, because she seemed worried.

"It is only this," I said very quietly. "I would be very gratified if you would call me by my first name."

"Oh! Is it not Rowan?" she asked, tilting her head to one side.

"No. Each knight, upon entering service, takes up a certain name," I said, and explained to her the convention, which she seemed quite surprised by. At the end, as she toyed with the free strands of her hair, she asked shyly,

"In that case—what *is* your first name?"

Fool that I am, I had nearly forgotten that I hadn't told her. Somehow I suppose I thought that she already knew, that she had some spell over me which had told her everything, not least how to look so perfectly irresistible.

"My name is Rhys," I told her, and she smiled as she repeated it back to me, sending shivers along my spine. I hadn't meant to crowd her, but I leant over her then, steadying myself against the door.

"Thank you, Rhys," she said again, "for helping me, and for

teaching me things I didn't know." And then once more she kissed me.

This time it was different. Her touch was so gentle and light, her body a hair's breadth from mine. And yet somehow she gave me such a powerful feeling of being felt and heard and seen, so that again I might have feared that she knew all my secrets, except for the fact that there was such sweetness in her too, as if some part of her was saying to me, *it will all turn out alright, Rhys; I know you for what you are.*

She bade me goodnight afterward, and I lay down outside her door as though I was making my bed in the stars.

P.S. It was a good thing I offered to sleep here and Daisy accepted—just now (very late into the night, I should think) I was awakened by one of the awful knightlings kicking my stomach in an attempt to get to the door. If there wasn't a storm outside I'd have him on the field at this moment! In fact I've half a mind to send him out there anyway. But I managed to send him away quietly for now; I do not think Daisy has awoken, thank goodness.

Twelve

A Desperate Meeting

Daisy

I had such a strange dream that night, after I'd kissed him—Rhys—and listened to him talk about commitments and duty. Of course I always knew knights considered themselves bound to a duty. I just had always assumed that duty was solely to mow down dragons and terrorize wild creatures. And yes, I know that sounds a little silly, but do knights ever think of a dragon's duty? Not that that's an excuse, but I hope you see my point.

Anyway, in my dream, I was at home with the Tree and the pixies, and they were all huddled up in their tiny homes, shivering. I was trying to keep them warm, but at the same time, I heard someone trying to get in to where we were. I couldn't go out to see who it was and fend them off without leaving the pixies to the cold. I thought all was lost, but then Rhys came, and stood between us, and fended off the strange attacker.

I only mention it because it turned out to be a little more relevant than I might have liked. When I got up that morning after kissing Rhys, I helped him make breakfast, and of course the other knights were there. It took a while for some of them to wake up, and even longer for them to come to the table. Actually in that way I thought they didn't seem too different from some of the pixies.

But their conversation was much worse. Rhys was questioning them about something—all of them, but especially the old one, Sir Perceval. I gathered that they had stayed behind in the woods on purpose the day before, and Rhys thought they might have had something to do with the storm. Finally, over pancakes and tea, Sir Perceval admitted that they *had* been up to something but what they had *meant* to do was *summon a dragon!*

"To help you find the Tree," he told Rhys. "We talked about this, lad."

I don't think Rhys shared Sir Perceval's opinion. I remembered, of course, what I had overheard Sir Perceval say about Sir Rowan's quest—that it'd be easier to find the dragon than the Tree. But I had thought they were just *looking.* I hadn't realized how much magic the knights might do.

"We had a bit of bad luck, though," Sir Perceval admitted. "Something was off. You may be right, Rowan, thinking we called down the snow. See, I got the idea from your description that it might be an ice dragon."

Sir Rowan thinks he has seen the dragon? I dropped the wooden bowl I was washing in the sink. Fortunately, I don't think any of the knights noticed. They were too busy plotting.

"Why would an ice dragon be guarding the Tree of Life?" Sir Rowan asked, and it was pretty clear he was gritting his teeth.

"That's what I said!" said one of the younger knights.

"It was just a first try," said Sir Perceval defensively. "We'll give it another shot as soon as the storm lets up."

"That was not my plan," Sir Rowan protested.

"Just let us try it, old chap," said Sir Lancelot. "What could the harm be?"

Other than frosting all my plants and scaring the horses out of their wits, I wondered. And I had to admit, I was nearly shocked out of my own wits as well. The only good thing about all this, as far as I could see, was that the storm seemed likely to last another day or more. I'd gone up to the first floor first thing that morning, and the snow banks were up to the windows, and the wind hadn't ceased.

That didn't stop the knights talking about it, though. They spent all morning plotting how they would do it.

At last I couldn't take it any longer. Rhys excused himself from their little circle, saying he had to go up to his room to retrieve some book, I think. As soon as he was gone I all but darted after him, saying I wanted to check the upstairs fireplaces for signs of the snow getting in.

There were two things on my mind. First, that I didn't want to fight anyone. Second, that the longer I kept my secret from Rhys, the more he might *want* to fight me over it.

I don't think I even knocked on his door. In fact I'm pretty sure I didn't, because I remember his eyes were wide as saucers when I shut his bedroom door behind me and began pacing like a trapped beast.

"I have to tell you two things," I said to him, trying my best to be as clear as possible. "The first is that I—I like you, and I don't want to fight you."

"My lady," he said, "you honor—"

"Hush a moment." I actually walked right up to him and put my finger over his lips, and stood there staring up at him as I rambled, "that was only the first thing. The second thing is that I *don't* like your friends, and I need you to help me stop them."

His brow creased and from behind my hand he said, "I had presumed as much, my lady, and if I thought that their plans would harm you, of course I would—"

"I'm the dragon," I interrupted, unable to bear the suspense. "They need to not find the dragon they want, because *I* am the dragon you're looking for."

There was a moment of silence. I took my hand away from his mouth. His face had gone very pale. He wavered a little, but didn't step away.

"*You* are the dragon?" he asked at last.

"Yes."

"You are a *dragon?*" His voice rose.

"Yes."

"You are *the* dragon?"

"Yes," I said, "but could you please be quiet about it?"

He did. In fact he sat down on the bed, and I began pacing again, going back and forth in front of him.

"I didn't mean to lie to you," I admitted. "But then, I didn't really want to tell you either, because of course you are a knight. I didn't know anything about you before you came. I didn't know that you wanted—"

He caught me then, his hands on my waist, and he pulled me down into his lap. He kissed me, pulling me in so close I couldn't deny him, his strength apparent as I leaned into his chest. His mouth on mine was hot, but he still tasted like snow. I had the giddy thought that perhaps *he* was an ice dragon, and wouldn't that be lovely, and solve all our problems.

Thirteen

New Thoughts

‿∾⟨∾⟩∾‿

Sir Rowan
  22nd Day of the 1st Moon

I don't care in the slightest what happened this morning. Sir Perceval indulging the knightlings' fantasies is all it was.

Everything shifted when Daisy told me who she truly is.

I sat there like an utter fool at first, because I hadn't had any suspicion. I still have to hear from her why she is able to take a different shape. But in retrospect so many other things make sense, like her imperviousness to the cold and her extreme wariness of knights in general.

But I wasn't thinking of that in the moment. I wasn't even thinking of the Tree or my quest. I was only thinking of her. She was apologizing—not that she had any reason to—and I thought to myself, knowing this, do I still feel that deep connection to her?

Of course I did. I kissed her just to be sure, and I admit I was a bit forward in doing so, but I think it was a very pertinent reminder. My lady certainly didn't seem to mind.

"Are you quite certain about all of this?" I asked her, just to tease her a little and see her smile at me rather than purse her lips. Her pretty face hung low and very close to mine.

I felt her little laugh as I held her body, and stroked my hand through her hair. "I am," she said, "though what I'm *not* certain about is why you don't seem to mind."

"My lady, I never thought I had a right to all your secrets," I told her, and kissed her forehead lightly as I added, "Nor am I easily swayed."

"Clearly." She returned my kiss, but then the worry returned to her voice. "Do you see now what I mean about the other knights, though? The last thing I want is to transform and get into some battle with them. We'd only end up knocking down the tower, and how will I explain that to Lavender? Not to mention that then, everyone would know about the pixies."

"I see," said I, although I still don't quite understand what she meant about pixies. "and I will aid you, of course. We will find a way around it; on that you have my word."

She pulled back and looked me over with that same careful air, which now made me smile. "I appreciate that. But afterward . . . what will you do about your quest?"

"I imagine I will want to ask you many questions," I said humbly, trying to gauge from her expression how willing she might be to talk to me.

"I . . . I've never told anyone about any of it," she admitted, her head tilted as she thought.

"And you need not feel you must tell me," I reminded her. "It is your decision, my lady. And you have time to consider it."

"Yes," she said absently, "I have to get back to the kitchen now, in any case. I only . . . well . . . I'm not sure exactly how to explain it. But—if we make it through this—I could at least tell you some things."

She left soon afterward, leaving me to the sound of the wind on the stones. I have remained here a while. It would not do to return right after her, after all, and there is much on my mind, so I decided to take these notes while it all was fresh.

What a strange twist of fate, that the woman who has ensnared me would also be the guardian of that which I seek, and other secrets besides. It only proves that it is true what they say, that the very best of plans are always broken. That she should be the one to stand between me and redemption . . . is redemption even necessary any more? Of course it must be; I can not leave matters unfinished. I have walked this path too long. Still, if she is to be the wall that blocks my path, I feel I could stop and rest awhile quite easily . . . is it wrong of me? Is this a failure? It doesn't feel the same as the mistakes I have made in the past. Nothing about her is a mistake. I can but keep my word to her, and see where it leads.

Fourteen

Fly and Find

Daisy

I'm not sure what I expected Rhys's reaction to be when I told him about myself, but I hadn't expected it to be a kiss. And not only a kiss, but a request to know more! I had feared he would be upset, and had thought that perhaps the most likely reaction would be a pulling back, a cooling off. But if anything he seemed more warm toward me than ever.

A part of me did think that maybe it was part of some scheme. That didn't seem likely at all, but of course, I didn't know him so well then, and I had centuries of thinking knights were awful at my back, so it was hard to be sure.

In any case, I told myself, *you have to focus on getting the other knights out and getting through the storm—not on how perfect his hand felt in your hair.*

It was too bad, I thought, that I didn't ask him—just to be sure—whether the other knights could tell who I am.

I was pretty certain by then that they couldn't. But even so I found their company very trying. It seemed forever before Rhys followed me down the stairs. When he finally came back to the kitchen, his glance at me went right through my soul. I tried very hard to pretend I was busy watering my plants.

And standing there at the window well is when I first felt it, underneath all the worry and the aching desire. It was a low hum, a sound that sang through my bones—something I hadn't heard or felt in a long time, not since Mother had flown off to join the Circle of Dragons, our worldwide council.

I realized that Sir Perceval had been more effective than he thought.

But how could I tell the knights without admitting how I knew?

Should I tell the knights?

I had to tell Rhys, at least. I turned toward the hearth, but he was busy showing one of the younger knights how to do something with swords. The firelight flickered off the metal and into their faces, and I remember being very frustrated at the time, because I just couldn't *imagine* playing with such silly sticks when a dragon was outside.

And coming closer.

The dragon's hum in my bones had changed to a roar. It had found what it wanted—found us, I supposed, though I wasn't sure what it had come for. A rumble from the tower walls answered that question quickly. I myself have never laid siege to a keep, but my brother has said often that the thing to do is go for the walls first, because it limits the knights' options and it makes the tower fall much more nicely afterward. Apparently this stranger agreed.

And it solved one of my problems, because I didn't have to tell the knights what was happening. They heard the noise, too, and they all leapt up.

"I'll go," Sir Lancelot said hurriedly. "It could be nothing."

"It could be a dragon," said Sir Perceval, and I almost forgot myself and agreed with him aloud.

"We will have no idea what it is until we look," said Rhys, and as the others rushed past him, he added, "Use caution!"

They stormed up the stairs, and I knew what they found would keep them busy. I ran across the room and caught Rhys by the wrist.

"It *is* a dragon," I told him. "I know it is, and it's going after the walls. I have to go out and—and intervene. I may have to chase it off. Sometimes they can be very determined. I'll have to go as myself, though, and *they can't see me change.*"

"Of course," he said very nicely, as though all of this made sense, though I know I was talking a mile a minute and he can't have understood half of it.

I tugged him across the kitchen, reaching into my room for a moment to grab my bag off its hook. "Take this," I told him, pushing it into his arms. "If anything—if anything happens to me—"

"My lady," he interrupted, "I will find you."

The next thing I remember I was in the air, circling the tower, and Rhys's words still echoed in my mind, just as though he rode upon my shoulder. I could see the other dragon—he was very large, an old ice dragon, just like I had thought Rhys might be. He was harrying the knights in the yard, playing with them. He was far too upset about the summoning to be reasoned with. Magic-tinged, that's what my mother used to call it. It messes up the senses. I've never felt it myself—maybe I'm so used to the pixies that I'm immune. But I know it can be very dangerous in others. Now that he had found the people who had done this to him, he wasn't going to leave them alone.

But I couldn't let him destroy Lavender's property and terrify the horses. And—though I didn't think it at the time—I couldn't let him hurt Rhys.

I will find you.

Fifteen

Fight and Drink

Sir Rowan
  22nd Day of the 1st Moon, cont.

And to think, when I left off earlier, I thought the day could hold no more surprises!

I hope devoutly that Sir Perceval and the others have learned their lesson today. The four of them ran right out into the yard, of course, and when I joined them I found them facing a fully-grown dragon without mounts, and *still* in a snowstorm. The battle might well have been over before it began. The dragon was massive, a glacier blue, with crackling spines and huge leathery wings that beat the snowdrifts into impenetrable fog. One fore claw as big as a horse rested upon a pile of rubble that had once been the front gate, and with its other clawed hand it swiped at the knights, sending them scattering. One fell over, and truthfully I think that was his good luck, because he disappeared into the fallen snow. The dragon focused on Sir Lancelot, who drew its gaze toward the stables.

Sir Lancelot is never at fault for shirking his duty in a fight, but I can't help but think it was folly to direct the dragon toward the horses. It only goes to show how little any of them were thinking.

I had only my sword; a lance would have been better, but I was glad to have anything on hand at all. I circled around the side of the yard, thinking I might get close enough to cut the dragon across its side. The move was foolish, for I had little shelter to fall back upon, but I had no choice: I wouldn't let the dragon find Nessie in his stall. I came up along the wall. But the broken rocks had iced over, whether from the storm or the dragon I couldn't say, and for a moment I was stymied.

In that moment, she came. She must have gone up into the clouds at first, and perhaps she did something to the storm itself, because as she came down, shafts of gray light came with her. The light caught in her wings and cast colors like stained glass all over the snow.

What she told me is true—not that I had any reason to doubt her, aside from my own ignorance. And furthermore, I realized then that *she* was the dragon I'd seen before. I'd been right.

And she is very beautiful.

She swooped very close over my head, a white shadow. In the moment I couldn't tell what had happened, but it soon became clear that she had taken the ice dragon by the scruff of its neck and bodily dragged it off of the wall. The ice dragon must have been twice her size. But by using her momentum and the element of surprise, she spared the knights and the horses.

After that, however, she had no surprise on her side. The ice dragon picked itself up and roared. She hovered over the trees, just barely visible. I knew she was making herself a target rather than the keep, but I feared for her then; her gossamer wings seem so fragile, and her slender claws were no match for the brutish ice dragon. I scrambled over the wall that had stopped me moments before, thinking to aid her. But I needn't have worried.

With another roar, the ice dragon launched itself into the air at her. But it was too near the ground to pick up speed, and deftly she rose above it before coming down upon its back. This time the ice dragon hit the ground and Daisy hovered between it and the keep. She'd traded places with it.

In the sudden triumph of it, the cleverness of her movement, I forgot myself and let out a glad shout. The ice dragon's head swiveled and it caught sight of me standing atop the broken wall. Shaking its spines and scraping through the snow, it began to charge right for me.

Again Daisy blocked it. She hurtled directly into the dragon this time, and they both went rolling through the snow and over the cliff beside the keep.

I clung to the wall, unable to breathe. I couldn't help thinking how easy it is to tear the wings of a dragonfly. But she rose; she rose, more slowly than before, but she came up first over the edge of the cliff. She had her back to me, and was looking down beneath her. I could have sobbed with relief. But my moment of weakness was interrupted by the sound of the other knights slipping over the rocks behind me. I ordered them back into the yard and they obeyed, perhaps thinking that I meant them to stay in safety. Not even Sir Lancelot questioned me, so desperate was the tenor of my voice.

Daisy, meanwhile, had settled onto the cliff and still looked below her. After a moment she growled, and then she let out a terrible roar, a sound that seemed to shake the very mountain beneath us. Like a chorus, the birds hiding in the forest answered her.

But the ice dragon did reappear. It climbed through the air clumsily, and I could have sworn something in its demeanor sneered down at Daisy. She leapt up, growling again, but she was just slightly too slow. The ice dragon knocked her back into the woods. But to do so sent it off balance, and though it seemed to glance back at the keep for just a moment, it quickly gave up on the notion of continuing its fight, choosing instead to fly painfully off into the clouds.

The storm had settled, and the birds called curiously. Daisy, however, did not rise. I immediately set to work. I sent the curious knightlings out after the ice dragon with orders only to watch it and see if it truly left. I myself saddled Nessie and rode directly for the place I'd seen Daisy fall into the trees.

She'd landed in a meadow—or at least I assumed as much, because the trees formed a ring around a wide crater in the snow. But in that crater, no white dragon lay; instead, I found my lady in her human form, curled up on her side on the ground, and utterly naked but for two necklaces slung round her throat.

I leapt down from Nessie before we stopped. Nessie kept going until it could poke its blue snout in my lady's hair, making her laugh weakly as I covered her in my cloak. I could tell from the way she moved as she struggled upright that she had not won her victory completely unharmed.

"It's my shoulder," she admitted, seeing my look. "I fell on it when we went over the cliff. And then I was trying to protect it when I came down just now, so I landed all wrong and hurt my knee, as well. But it isn't so bad, all in all. Did you bring my bag with you?"

I handed the bag to her; as it turned out, she had been prepared for just this eventuality. The bag had a change of clothes in it, down to a pair of soft boots. I held my cloak out for her as a screen while she began to pull on her clothes. It soon became apparent from her labored breathing, however, that this was unsustainable.

"My lady," I entreated, "I wonder if perhaps you would let me assist you."

She paused for a moment, and then sighed. "I suppose you might as well."

I lowered my cloak just enough to see her face. "Would it be so bad, my lady?"

"I didn't mean that. It's only that I . . ." She blushed, and sagged a little further on her one good leg. "I'm not exactly like a normal human, even . . . like this."

I didn't fully understand this yet, and the doubt in her voice was not permission. So I hesitated.

After another moment she sighed again, and smiled at me despite the wariness in her eyes. "I'm not *totally* immune to the cold," she said, trying to make her voice light. "Will you—would you please help me, Rhys?"

Not having realized that this was the case, I dropped my cloak and set to work at once. She stood in her underwear, balancing on her boots. At first I was so focused on untangling her leggings from her other clothes that I didn't recognize what she had alluded to earlier.

I knelt in the snow at her feet and she leant on my shoulder as I helped her with the leggings. As I rose I kept my hands on her hips. Very gently, I turned her body so that I could check her shoulder, and that's when I understood why she'd hesitated.

"It isn't broken," she murmured. "I think I might have torn a muscle, is all."

"The bruising has already started," I observed as I looked back at her face. The entirety of her left shoulder blade was covered in deep, angry bruises, explaining why her arm hung awkwardly. Her one good hand, I noticed, was clutching at one of her necklaces. I longed to draw her into me, to kiss her as I ran my fingers down her back, along the white scales that traced her spine.

Instead I sifted through the rest of her bag. We agreed to avoid the bra she'd packed, as it would only give her pain. Instead I settled an old sweater over her bare skin. She didn't try to hide anything from me. But she did keep her hand on that old locket on its gold chain around her neck. Her other necklace, a clear crystal on a woven string, cast faint rainbows on her pale skin.

"It's one of the things about—who I am that never changes," she said as I helped her unhurt arm into its sleeve.

I assumed she referred to the scales, and—motivated by a desire to keep her talking, to distract her—I asked what the other unchanging things might be as I tried very gently to ease her injured arm into the sweater.

"Um," she murmured at first, hissing faintly at the pain before recovering and smiling at me to continue. "I have very light bones. But they're very strong, too—that's how I know, or at least I think, that I haven't broken anything." She swayed against me as I pulled the hem of the sweater down and I caught her, concerned. "Oh no—don't worry. It's fine. It's just that I am—tired. Changing . . . takes a lot of energy."

69

"Not only changing form, but saving the keep and everyone in it," I reminded her. She smiled up at me and, boldened, I said, "I am glad you have those qualities, my lady. It will make this much easier."

"This?" she asked, puzzled.

"May I carry you?" I returned mildly. She understood, and though I think normally she might have shied away, she very gracefully acquiesced. Careful not to hurt her, I gathered her into my arms—she *is* very light—and held her to my chest as I mounted Nessie, who had become rather impatient waiting for us.

"He might come back," she murmured as we paced through the trees.

"Don't worry, my lady." I kissed the top of her head. "We will be more prepared next time."

As luck would have it, we returned to the keep before the others. I was able to lay my lady down in her bed and convince everyone else that she had been inside the keep the entire time, and was sleeping off the shock.

While the day was still light, Sir Lancelot and his knightlings resolved to make the trip to town—to warn the people about the ice dragon, and keep a further lookout if necessary. I doubted it would be, because dragons rarely attack towns without provocation, but I was very glad of the excuse to reduce our party. Sir Perceval stayed with Daisy and me.

Though the storm had broken, we lingered in the kitchen—myself to be near Daisy, and Sir Perceval, I think, to be near me. It is possible he noticed something odd in my behavior; or perhaps he simply felt guilty for his part in the dragon's appearance. But he was good company, if not quite the company my heart desired. And he was convivial when

Daisy made her reappearance near dinner time.

"Hello Sir Perceval, hello Sir Rowan," she said, her voice still a little weary. But her small smile shone from the shadows near her room. "I'm sorry to have slept so long."

"Daisy, there you are," said Sir Perceval gaily, waving a hunk of the roast from last night. He'd been snacking steadily despite my preparations for dinner, saying that he could not stand to wait for food. "You're just in time, lass, don't worry."

I started toward her at once, because I understood why she was not crossing the room herself. It must have hurt her very much to walk. "My lady, I have just started dinner. You may find it prudent to allow me to tend your injuries while we wait for it to cook."

She looked up at me uncertainly, and I could hear Sir Perceval's snort of surprise behind me as well. For both their benefit, I said, "Miss Daisy hurt herself in the fray earlier, attempting to run through the garden over the ice."

Sir Perceval accepted this at once, and even commended my lady for her narrow escape. She in turn saw what I had done and smiled her acquiescence, and nodded as I moved to lift her up. It was difficult to carry her without hurting either her shoulder or her knee, as the injuries are on opposite sides of her body, and her knee had swollen up a great deal by then. Fortunately, the walk was short. I placed her on the counter along the outer wall, near the table at which Sir Perceval sat, and at once I began making some remedies for her. I had intended to do so the moment she woke up, and so I had many of the ingredients prepared already; I only had to finish the process.

"What are you doing?" Daisy asked curiously as I began heating water and combining ingredients for her tisane.

"That's what he does," Sir Perceval replied before I had a chance to. I let him speak, so that I could focus. "He mixes drinks and things. Famous for it among knights. Whatever he gives you, lass, I advise you drink it, because it's bound to help."

Daisy's head tilted to one side as she watched me, brushing unruly tendrils of hair from her face. "So it's like medicine?"

"I make no pretensions to science," I told her, "because a great deal of my successes, such as they are, are unrepeatable."

"So . . . is it magic, then?" she asked.

"As a rule, I prefer not to meddle in magic," I assured her, because it seemed to me there was an undertone of worry in her words. After the ice dragon she'd had to battle today, I couldn't blame her.

"It's old fey tricks," said Sir Perceval from his place at the table. "That's what some people say. That he learned it from his time with the water fairies, not that he'd ever tell—"

"Is that true?" Daisy asked me, her eyes round and interested.

"Yes," I told her, much to Sir Perceval's surprise. Ignoring his sputtering, I told her what I'd never confessed to anyone else. "While I served in the court of the water fairies, their cook taught me these recipes. When they died, they left all their notes to me. I only endeavor to follow in their footsteps."

Daisy watched me with that careful look on her face, though it was animated too by sympathy, I thought. Most likely she knows that fairies do not die of natural causes. But she was too good to ask me about it then, and admittedly I gave her little opportunity, for the moment the tisane was ready, I brought it to her in a steaming mug and insisted she drink.

"Very well, then," she said, smiling first at me and then at Sir Perceval. While I turned to preparing the next remedies, he told her all about the fight—not realizing of course that she had been part of it—and where the others had gone. Though she chatted with him amiably enough, I often thought I felt her eyes on my back. I couldn't turn to look at her; I would have lost all hope of concentration if I had.

I had just finished preparing the poultice for her knee when at last Sir Perceval rose and said he would stay upstairs for the evening. "We've got the fire up there going again," he told Daisy, "and I'll be comfortable enough. I figure I'll keep an eye out for any signs of dragons or other passersby. And I'll leave you," he said to me, "to your lady." I rather think he winked as he said it.

Daisy watched him go with an amused look on her face, and when the door to the stairway had fully closed, she said, "I suppose all knights *aren't* so bad, are they."

"I should hope not," I murmured, watching her.

She turned to me and smiled. "I already knew you weren't. I have finished the tea you gave me. What is that you have now?"

I explained the remedy to her and inquired about her leggings—whether they were loose enough to be folded back above her knee.

"Yes," she said, pausing just a moment to think about it. "I hate to put you to so much trouble, though."

"Think nothing of it," I insisted. Setting her foot up on the back of a chair, cushioned on an old towel, I folded back the leggings I had helped her into mere hours before. She did not speak, but kept her eyes on me; I wonder if she could tell how difficult I found it to keep steady.

After wrapping her knee and placing a bowl beneath it in case of drips, I finally allowed myself to look at her face. She was beautiful, the inarguable beauty of a fierce creature caught in a vulnerable state. It took everything in me not to cover her in kisses, or to weep.

Instead I turned to poke at the fire, shifting coals over the oven which slowly cooked our shepherd's pie.

"There is your shoulder, as well," I said hesitantly as I returned to the counter.

"If you can't do anything for it, that's alright," she said. "It will heal in time."

"But my lady, I hate to see you in pain." I cleared my throat. "There are several things I could try. However . . ."

"It'd be easiest if I took off my shirt?" she guessed, smiling crookedly at me. "It's okay, I thought that might be the case. I—if it's only you here with me, then—then I think that would be alright."

"In that case I will begin preparations at once," I said, turning back to my herbs and bottles. This time I talked to her as I worked, because it was unbearable not to be near her somehow. I asked her what she thought Mme Lavender's reaction might be.

"I'm sure she'll be kind about it," said Daisy, thoughtfully. "She won't blame anybody about it. But she'll probably want to get it fixed before renting again."

"I haven't deprived you of income, have I?" I realized at once that no renters might mean no job or money for her.

"No," she said at once, easing my racing heart. "Why would you say that? Why would you say *you* had done it? It was the others who sommuned an ice dragon."

"But it was I who brought them here and made them complicit in my quest," I countered.

For a moment Daisy was silent. Then she said gently, "You are awfully quick to take blame for things, aren't you. Is that part of being a knight?"

I hadn't expected this, and had no answer at first. I stuttered, much like Sir Perceval had earlier. "I believe in taking full responsibility for my own actions," I said finally.

"Hmm." Daisy thought. "And is that why you have been kind to me? Is that why you are helping me now?"

"No," I said immediately. "On the contrary, my lady, I am helping you because—because, as you aptly said, I like you."

Was it only this morning she said those words? They have already etched a place in my heart.

When I glanced over she was blushing, and when she spoke, there was laughter in her voice, as though she was a little embarrassed but also pleased. "That's all right, then," she decided.

"The poultice is almost ready," I said, glad for the distraction. But as I moved to her, to help her remove her sweater, I worried. "We could cut it, my lady," I offered, more than once. But she insisted it wasn't necessary, despite her wincing. Very, very carefully, I helped her out of it, at last sliding the fabric away from her injured arm.

I gave the sweater back to her, so that she could cover her front with it, but first she pressed it to her eyes. I felt at once I was rooted to the spot. "My lady—please—you aren't—?"

"It's nothing," she assured me, her voice light despite a small sob escaping. "It isn't what you think. It's not because of my shoulder. It's just that . . ." she looked up at me, and smiled very softly. I couldn't help myself; I took one of the sleeves from the sweater and gently brushed the tears from her cheeks. Then I lifted her hand and kissed it.

She shuddered. "Rhys," she murmured, "my shoulder. Whatever it is you wanted to do . . . I trust you."

I'm ashamed to say I stood for a moment, like a statue. I didn't quite understand her manner; in fact I still don't. But her words were sweeter than a siren's song to my ears.

I applied the poultice, and though it didn't do as much good as the one on her knee, it did seem to help. While it was working she let me dig through her clothes, and mine, so that I could help her don a light sleeveless undershirt. After the poultice was done and I put her arm in a sling, I wrapped one of my shawls around her. She smiled up at me, her hair so bright and her eyes so dark against the blue cloth.

That is when I truly kissed her. I stood there at the counter, her face cupped in my hands, her body pressing into mine, and I kissed her as deeply as I could, not realizing how hungry I had been, not caring how needy I was. Everything about her reminds me of sunlight and deep-rooted magic.

I suppose now I know why.

Sixteen

Telling Tales

Daisy

That night I think Rhys had a hard time concentrating. He was trying to write in his notebook while I tended my plants, but every moment or two he would get up and get something for me, or move something out of my way, or steady me as I swayed on my one good leg. I never asked him to do these things at first. But by the end of the evening, I did ask him to help me clean up.

It's not that I didn't like it—I just wasn't used to it. *I'm* used to being the one looking after sick pixies and ailing plants. I rarely if ever get hurt, in part because I usually avoid fighting as much as I can.

It didn't escape me that evening that what I was fighting the hardest was my attraction to him.

After we'd had dinner—Rhys thought it was burnt because he'd forgotten all about it while kissing me, but I thought it was fine—and I'd done everything I could think of to do, especially in my state, I finally let myself settle down on the bench beside him. We looked into the fire together, and—we talked.

I started it by asking about the water fairies. "I've never met a fairy," I admitted.

He seemed a little hesitant, like if he had any less restraint, he might have told me not to bother meeting any fairies in the future. I was already laughing a little when he finally looked up and chuckled.

"Pray do not attach much importance to my hesitation, my lady," he said. "My relationship with the clan I served was . . . a complicated one. I have not had much cause to discuss it with anyone."

"You don't have to if you don't want to," I assured him, but it was clear he was already thinking it over.

"It only very recently came to an end," he said softly, looking into the fire. He told me all about the rivalry between the water fairies and the ice fairies. He told me, too, about the fairy named Snow with her parents from different sides, and her friends the miners. And most touchingly, he told me about himself.

"Much of it was born of my mistake," he told me, his voice heavy. "Had I but advised her parents differently, so much of this could have been avoided."

I thought about this. I wondered if perhaps this was the burden of guilt which he'd been carrying, that made him so reserved sometimes. But it seemed too fresh for that. I said, "I wonder if it *could* have been, though. Often with the pixies it happens—they have their little dramas, and sometimes I try to intervene on behalf of one or another, but usually the end result is the same as it would have been if I had never spoken at all. I don't think it's because I give poor advice. I think it's because pixies are very stubborn little creatures. Maybe fairies are similar?"

"I think it likely that most beings are similar, my lady," he said with a crooked smile. "But that does not excuse my own callousness."

"Maybe not," I agreed. "But you know better, now."

He mulled this over for a moment, but soon changed the conversation. "You deal often with the pixies, my lady?"

I paused. He knew I was guardian of the Tree, but he didn't know why or who else lived with me.

"You don't have to tell me," he said, echoing what I had said earlier. "I only ask because of an old story I have heard."

"Tell me the story," I said, shifting to focus on his face.

He told me a tale of Gold-Tree and Silver-Tree, a thing I had never heard before, though I did know those names. "I haven't heard that story," I told him honestly, "and I will ask them about it. I promise. I—I can't tell you about them, not really, because that isn't my place. But I can ask for you."

He looked at me then so deeply, his blue eyes so focused on mine, that I thought he'd probably figured everything out right at that moment. It scared me a little, even though I knew it shouldn't, because he was a good person and had gone to such lengths to be kind to me. It's just that I had never told anyone before. It was my duty not to tell anyone.

"Thank you, Daisy," he said very seriously. And he smiled at me, and he talked about lighter things, and made me feel at ease. But I still worried in the back of my mind. Because if I messed up, it could lead to a fight, or worse, for the pixies.

And like I said, usually I avoid fighting. Usually I avoid everything. That's what I realized that night, that made me cry. I always avoided anything where anyone would have to care for me, never knowing why I was doing so. And then here was this man being so excruciatingly gentle that it made me cry just because of how tender he was, and how much he cared.

It didn't help that despite everything, we were still on opposite sides of a spectrum. I thought about that, long after I'd bade him goodnight. I lay awake looking at the ceiling, trying to picture a way in which a dragon with a duty and a knight with a quest could be friends.

Seventeen

Dissension in the Ranks

Sir Rowan
  23rd Day of the 1st Moon

My lady was not quick to rise the next morning, and no wonder. In fact I was pleased that she was getting some rest at last. I believe I might even have been humming as I set about stoking up the fire and preparing some breakfast things.

Ah, but I should have known that the moment of peace could not last long!

Sir Perceval, who had indeed been keeping a watchful eye over the walls—as well he ought!—was the first to bring the news. He broke in on my peaceful kitchen, his face flushed and out of breath. "They're coming," was all he said at first.

"Who is coming?" I asked, fearing dragons.

"The knights," he said, reaching for coffee. "They're coming back."

This gave me pause. I had expressly told Lancelot and the others to guard the village. I must confess, I had not thought for a moment that they would disobey me. I had rather expected that the confrontation with the ice dragon would have taught them what comes of that.

As I heard their voices at the door above, I realized for the first time that perhaps I had done a *truly* foolish thing in bringing them here. More foolish than subjecting myself to their bickerings and more foolish than dabbling in magic—more foolish, even, than inconveniencing my lady. It occurred to me, for the first time, that Sir Lancelot, with his dedication to quests and strong blac-and-white morals as applied to anyone but himself, might make exactly the wrong kind of foe. Especially now that I wanted nothing more than to quietly help my lady heal.

"Tally ho, all," he said as he and his knightlings swept into the kitchen. I remember because it was particularly stupid. And it made me think of hunting. "Lavender says we all need to come back to town."

"She sent us up here to get you," the knightlings agreed in chorus.

Well, that wasn't as bad as I'd feared. I sighed as I watched them devour the breakfast I'd been laying out.

"We can make the tavern our new base of operations," said Sir Lancelot to me. "Don't worry—we aren't giving up yet."

They would be, if I had anything to say about it, but I let that go. I know when to pick my battles, and at that moment, Daisy was my priority. It emphatically would *not* help her healing if she woke up and found herself besieged by knights.

I sent them upstairs to round up all of our things and check for storm damage, promising I'd join them in the main hall quite soon. Then, very deliberately, I waited until they'd finished tromping up the stairs before I went and knocked on my lady's door.

"My lady," I assured her, "it is only me."

"I thought so," she replied quietly, swinging her door open only so far as to let me in, and then swinging it shut behind me. Leaning one shoulder against the heavy wooden frame, she contemplated me with tired eyes. "I heard them come in. Thank you for sending them upstairs."

"I'm afraid they won't be satisfied unless I return with them this morning," I said, my words slightly rushed as I made an effort to get the sentence out without immediately taking it back. I found I couldn't quite meet her eye.

My lady was still watching me, her head against the door, her hair mussed. "Do you want to leave?"

She asked like she was genuinely curious—like she was curious with herself, too, for wondering.

"No," I answered promptly. "I do not like to leave you, especially not in this state. But I see no way around it; Lancelot said Lavender herself had suggested this, no doubt because she does not want anyone else to come to harm in her keep. It is sensible on her part. And . . . it was my action that brought the knights here in the first place, and as such I do have a duty to them. I have to get them to see that this quest is at an end."

"But it isn't," my lady pointed out, her brow creasing.

"It is, so far as they are concerned," I said. I did not add, *it is too dangerous to keep them here,* but I was certainly thinking it, and that must have shown on my face.

"Of course I will be glad to see them go," she said, as if agreeing with me, "but I—but you—"

"I am going no farther than Belville," I assured her. "My lady, I know it may be asking too much, but is there any way you could meet me there?"

She leaned up to stand straight, biting her lip as she toyed with the necklaces beneath her sweater. "I—I don't often go that far."

"Are you worried about discovery?" I guessed.

"Hm? Oh, no, not in the way you mean," she said. After a moment, she pulled out one of her pendants—the crystal one—and held it up to me. "The magic that helps me change form is very strong. I don't think there's anything out there that would detect it. But . . . with the ice dragon, and the knights, and everyone so close . . ."

I was about to say something, to suggest that I would find *her* somehow, anywhere she liked, when she interrupted her own train of thought.

"Of course, I do owe you answers," she said. "Even if it's just a yes or no. And I will have to talk to Lavender, about the keep. So I think—yes—I will try to meet you."

I wasn't so sure that sat well with me, that she would be visiting only out of a sense of duty, not of desire. But every moment I seemed to feel the weight of the other knights pressing at my back, and I wanted so badly to know that I'd see her again under *any* circumstance that I let the matter rest. Instead of probing or making her another offer, I felt all I had time for was a quick, gentle embrace, and an assurance that I would wait for her at Mme Lavender's.

And that is why now, this evening, having neither seen nor heard anything from her all day, I am very displeased with myself.

Eighteen

Beautiful Dreams

Sir Rowan
  24th Day of the 1st Moon

It has been an abysmal day.

And yet, I don't see what about it I could have changed—what about it I *would* change. I will wait for Daisy forever, whether she comes or not; there isn't anything else to be said on that subject. (Aside from the fact that I do wish very much that she *would* come, and I wonder if I should be worried about her health.)

There is a great deal, however, to be said about Lancelot.

He spouts all the ideals, chivalry and code and adventure and duty, but I find it more and more difficult to consider him a fellow knight. I have noted how little I myself feel like a knight any more. But whatever *I* am, broken as I may be, I am not the automata he is. Everything he says to me sounds hollow. I hear no conviction in him, except the ultimate conviction that I ought to agree with what he says.

We nearly came to blows over it this afternoon. I told them yesterday that I considered the quest over, of course. First I told them that I'd reconsidered my aims, which was actually quite near the truth; and when this didn't satisfy, I began increasingly making things up. First I told them I was stricken with guilt over the ice dragon affair, which was at least partially true. Then I said I had recognized a duty to the town of Belville, to keep it safe. This at least kept them quiet through the evening, but then in the morning they did not leave, and at last Sir Lancelot came and found me whilst the others ate lunch.

"We *can't* go," he said to me, sitting unwelcome beside me on the bench outside the tavern. "We *have* to see this through."

He kept repeating this, and slowly it morphed into *you have to see things through,* which I recognized as a jab at my own recent termination from the clan's employment. That was when I began to get angry.

"You absolutely *can* go," I retorted. "Your horses are well, despite how little care you give them; your gear is good, whether or not you deserve such finery; and your party is lively—far better it be lively somewhere else. In fact, what you can not do, Sir Lancelot, is stay here."

"Are you giving yourself airs?" Lancelot sneered at me. This, of course, is a knight's code for thinking above one's station, or becoming a liability. Knights with airs aren't just annoying; they're dangerous. In fact, they're often brought up in front of the Court.

"I am the one who invited you here," I returned coldly, "and I am saying this adventure is at an end."

"We came for you, surely, but not at your beck and call," he retorted. "And we've a right to stay anywhere we please."

"You have no right to cause trouble where you're not wanted," I said, and I must admit I was getting a bit desperate.

"*You'd* know a thing or two about being unwanted, I expect," he said, and it was clear in his face that he enjoyed his cruelty.

I can put an impassive face on in most circumstances, but I can not stand a bully. And neither can I stand to be reminded of the past—not now, with some wish of a future growing in my heart.

So I admit I took it too far. I stood. "You, *Sir* Lancelot, would know nothing at all. You do not see what is right in front of your face. What good would it do you to stay in town and look for the Tree of Life? You would not know it if you found it. You do not know me, and I doubt very much that you know yourself. In fact, in my opinion, you are the most self-involved, mindless glory hunter alive in the world today, and it was my mistake to *ever* so much as pen your name in connection with this quest."

Well, of course, after that, there was no answer but to duel. We're to meet outside of town tomorrow at daybreak.

I don't regret any of it . . . but I must say, I wonder what good is duty, when it makes shadows of people like me, and bright shining stars of vapid, changeable goons like them.

Nineteen

Honor and Glory

Sir Rowan
   25th Day of the 1st Moon

It is just before dawn, and I must ride out to meet Sir Lancelot. But if this be the end of my journal—for I am certain he will insist on dueling to the death—I did not want it to end on such a note.

Let it end, instead, with a recognition that I was trying to change. I do not know if it is for better or worse, but for once I have tried to own my mistake, and to speak up. And to love, though I am not so sure I had any choice in that matter.

My lady—forgive me.

Twenty

Interrupting Dragon

Daisy

Lavender gave me more money than she should have for looking after the knights, and I did get the pixies their yarn. They made me a very lovely pink and yellow shawl out of it. But somehow, I still felt cold.

The pixies helped me heal, too. It's something they can do only if they all come together in a big ritual, and only for people they think are important—so really, usually just themselves. They all join hands and they dance around the Tree, and they do some other things I don't fully understand. It takes some time, but they did it for me.

Of course they wanted to know all about how I'd been injured, and they were very cross with me when I didn't tell them everything. The eldest of the pixies, one everyone else calls Sha, even told me she could feel Rhys's magic on me. But

I told her that was silly because he didn't *use* magic, not really, and I tried my best not to let them see that even though they'd healed my injuries, a part of me still hurt.

I did ask Goldy Rhys's question, of course. Goldy is the third eldest of the pixies, and even though there isn't officially a leader, she's the one everyone looks to eventually for approval. She's always very bright and happy, and just as gold-colored as her name suggests. Naturally, she said I could tell him anything—"naturally," I say, because that was how *she* put it, as though she thought somehow it was my duty to tell things to Rhys. Nothing could have been farther from the truth, the way I saw it, but I couldn't convince her of that. She simply waved me away, laughing. Pixies can be like that. I suppose one of the reasons they have me is so that I can do some of their worrying for them.

I should have gone to see Rhys then. I had told him that I would. I felt terrible for not going—I ached to see him, and at the same time I felt exactly like what the pixies call a "pinky-swear breaker." But every time I thought of it—which was often—I couldn't think of how to do it, or what to say that would answer his questions but not make him ask more. Goldy's permission had honestly confused me. And I was scared, truthfully, that Rhys's quest was so important to him that I wouldn't be able to stop him trying to find the Tree, no matter what answers I gave him.

A strange fear, when you think of what happened next!

It started, of course, with the pixies. They came to me one morning and they said they could feel magic being done in the woods, "spells with ill intent," they called it. It was making them jittery and miserable with nerves. So I told them I'd go out and check to see what was happening on the mountain, and that in the meantime they ought to seal up our home with their magic very carefully as soon as I'd left.

I couldn't sense what they were talking about myself, but I did have a foreboding feeling that I knew where it might come from. I figured it *had* to be the knights again. So I decided to check the tower first, even though they weren't supposed to be staying there anymore, and after that I'd go check on the mine just in case.

It was a very overcast day—not terribly stormy like the days before, but dim and gray. I flew through the clouds, hiding myself as I peered down at the trees. Snow cover is actually very nice when you're looking for something from the air—as long as whatever you're looking for isn't white or brown or gray. I was pretty certain that I'd be able to spot the knights with their bold clothes and shiny armor.

But I didn't see them at first. I *heard* it first—the sound of metal crashing into metal, and hooves pounding the hard ground.

Well, I don't listen to all my brother's stories for nothing. I got an idea pretty quickly that it must be the knights, and that they must be fighting something. And in order to run with their horses like that, they had to be in a flat part of the forest. I flew down to a ledge, following the noises.

They didn't notice me coming through the clouds. But I was so surprised at first that I almost fell out of the air, and they would have noticed me *then*. The knights weren't fighting something. They were fighting *each other.*

At once I worried for Rhys. I came down closer over the trees, and I found Nessie easily. Rhys was astride him, tilting with a long lance against a red knight—Lancelot, I think. It didn't matter to me at all at the time. I could see the other knights, also on their horses, waiting and watching from under the trees. As Rhys and his attacker rode at each other, one of the other knights darted out from the cover of the trees and struck Rhys hard in the side without him having any idea that the blow was coming.

Rhys fell back, nearly sliding off his horse. I bellowed as loud as I could, enraged. I scared all the horses except Nessie, and they all set to rearing and running under the trees, giving me room to come down. The knights were all shouting and they probably wanted to fight me, but I didn't care. I pulled Rhys out of his saddle and cradled him close to my chest. I knew that Nessie, as a magic water horse, would surely find his master no matter where I took him. And so I cried out again at the other knights, and flicked their stupid sticks away, and disappeared into the clouds. And then I flew straight home.

This maybe sounds like a very silly thing to do—for a guardian of a secret place to carry a knight straight *to* that place. But he had been hurt very badly, so badly that he did not answer me when I spoke to him, even though I *knew* that he ought to hear me. And the pixies were worried and I had to get back to them as soon as possible. The knights were the source of the bad magic, I was sure of it. But I didn't want to go back and fight them with Rhys injured, and neither could I leave him in some abandoned tower or snowy cave. I'd learned that lesson in the stable during the snowstorm: knights are not impervious to cold.

I could only hope that Nessie disliked the other knights as much as I did, and wouldn't lead them to my home.

The pixies put up layers of protection around their home, especially the entrance to it. But I am not affected by any of the magic, because they have marked me somehow. I flew right through their illusions and shields and I glided down the tunnel, weary from carrying a knight *and* his heavy armor. I finally collapsed to the ground just at the edge of the rounded cave that the pixies call home.

They'd known I was coming, of course, and at once they were all over me, clamoring to see Rhys. They wanted to touch him, and poke him, and steal little pieces of his hair and tunic and anything that wasn't metal. I let him down gently onto the ground beneath me and they swarmed us both until I finally had to roar at them to make them back up.

"You *must* keep your distance," I told them, and all their little eyes were big and bright as stars looking back at me. "He is not bad. But he is very badly hurt. I have to tend him. If he is still here in the morning, you can meet him then."

I said all this very loudly, to show them I meant it, and I suppose because of that I woke him up. I heard him groan beneath me, and—after glancing round at the pixies again to make sure they would be nice—I shifted, and leaned down to say,

"Rhys, can you understand me?"

He looked up and my heart melted because I could see from his creased brow that he was in pain. But he nodded, so I went on,

"Everything is going to be okay. You'll be fine. Just rest for a moment, and I'm going to change into a human so I can help you."

He closed his eyes and I made the transformation quickly, calling on the power within my crystal. Remembering his concern about propriety, I darted over the mossy ground to pick up some clothes from where I'd stashed them amongst the Tree's roots. I pulled them on as I ran back over to him.

The pixies, those who hadn't already lost interest, hovered in a semicircle all around him, watching.

"Rhys," I said again, this time tumbling onto my elbows leaning over his face. He opened his eyes at once and tried to smile at me. "Rhys, I don't know if you remember all that happened, but I think you must be very badly hurt along your side."

"Not . . . exactly, my lady," he said, his voice quiet and hoarse. "It is my hip, I fear. The force of the blow . . . knocked me back . . . wasn't prepared . . ."

"Yes, I saw it," I agreed. I pursed my lips. "What can we do? You have to tell me. None of us here know very much about human medicine, but I can make things if you tell me how."

I think he meant to laugh, but the sound was weak. "My lady, I'm afraid . . . there's not much to be done . . . without a cast or framework to keep it steady . . . but we have no wood . . ."

I realized then that he couldn't see anything but my face and the ceiling of the cave, which is always obscured in hundreds of multi-colored lights. "Rhys," I said softly, "look up. Look behind you."

He did so slowly, tilting his head against the ground beneath him. I could tell the moment he caught sight of it, his face transformed with wonder.

"I am sure somehow its magic can help you," I insisted. I *needed* this to be true, because I couldn't ask the pixies to heal him when they'd never be able to focus and their spells took so long in any case. "I only need you to tell me how to get that magic to you. Should you drink it? Should I—should I make a poultice, like you did before?"

"Never thought . . . to use it on myself . . ." He slid his head back down and closed his eyes, thinking, half smiling to himself before finally clearing his throat. "My lady, could you spare a long strip of its bark, or perhaps a root? I think . . . I believe if we were to use it like . . . hmm . . . if you think of it as a bandage, wrapped—"

"I understand," I said, seeing what he meant to convey. "You stay here. Don't move. I'll be right back."

I got up and ran to the line of pixies, finding Sha and Goldy and the one other elder, Bree, so I could consult with them. They were as curious as the rest of them, but they could see I had no time to waste in games. All three of them agreed to what Rhys had suggested, much more readily than I expected.

I had to confer, too, with the Tree itself—and that part is hard to explain. It is not like a conversation, but a trading of feelings. I put my hand on its trunk and there was knowledge there, and willingness. As I cut I could feel its pain, too, but it gave me a great sense of peace as well.

I raced back to Rhys as soon as I could. In my absence he *had* moved, a little, trying to remove his armor and clothes. I saw this and took over for him at once, but it was very frustrating work with lots and lots of buckles and buttons. I *hate* little fiddly things like that.

Finally I got the skin of his leg and hip exposed, which was a very terrible sight to see. I don't think the bones of his thigh were in their right places at all, and he was bruised up to his ribs, even though he said that wasn't the most important thing to worry about. When I started wrapping his leg he passed out very quickly, which made me nervous but in retrospect was a good thing. The bark from the Tree began glowing as I laid it over his skin. When I'd wrapped as much as I could, laying the free end up along his side, I waited for a moment—and wished very hard, because as my mother would always say, 'there's magic, yes, but wishing never hurts.'

There was a blaze of light and there, under my hands, his body changed.

At once I dropped my hold on the bark and leant over his face again, calling his name.

And at last, his beautiful blue eyes opened, and he smiled and put his hand on my cheek. "You have saved me, Daisy," he said. And then he pulled my head down between his hands and kissed me so hard I forgot all about the pixies and the Tree.

After a moment, as he kissed me he began to lean up, shifting slowly so that he ended up sitting with me in his lap, his once-injured leg under mine.

"My lady," he murmured, resting his forehead against mine. He repeated, "I would be lost, and worse, without you."

"Maybe," I agreed, twisting so that I could look up at him, "but I still don't understand how we ended up here. I have so many questions, Rhys."

"Ask me everything," he said softly, placing a kiss in my hair.

This made me giggle a little, as though I was very young, and I couldn't explain it except that I felt so very warm and safe wrapped up in his arms like that. Not to mention that, despite all my belief in the Tree, I was so incredibly relieved that its bark had worked so well.

But I did my best to focus and be practical. There were still the pixies to think about, and Rhys's comfort. He was still mostly unclothed around the waist.

"I will," I said, in answer to him, "but perhaps first you should dress, and then—then I need to get some things from my quarters, and I should take you back to the tower, if you don't mind. Are you still hurt at all? Are you hungry?" *He and the knights must have left town early to be battling up on the mountain,*

I thought.

"Ravenous, but otherwise well," Rhys agreed, kissing me once before he released me. "I would be glad to make something for the both of us, my lady. Take me wherever you like."

I smiled at him. "Perfect. Just give me a moment—I'll be right back."

I ran back over to the circle of waiting pixies, who clamored for my attention. But I only spoke to the Elders, and that just for a moment, to be sure they were okay with everything I planned.

"You are connected," Sha kept saying to me, using the pixie term for lifelong companions, "connected ones."

"I only just met him—but I know he won't hurt you," I said, trying to both brush off her implications and reassure her at the same time. I think she knew more than I told her, because she let me go very quickly. All three of them did.

When I came back to Rhys, he was dressed in the breeches that go beneath his mail, and a loose white shirt. Before that day I had never seen him without all his armor and fancy tunic on, and I suppose I hadn't realized how many layers knights wear. *And still they get cold!* I suppose I was looking at him funny—it *was* a very intimate feeling, I realized, knowing what he wears beneath his outer clothes—because he cleared his throat and gestured at the pile of armor at his feet.

"I thought it best to discard it, for now," he said, "if my lady does not mind? I will of course take it away later. But not all of the pieces are fully functional."

"Oops." I thought back to my frustration with all the buckles.

He smiled. "The bulk of the damage was not done by you, my lady, but by the blow that knocked me back against the saddle and dented armor I had assumed was impenetrable."

"We can sort it out later, in any case," I assured him, reaching out my hand. "Come with me—if you would like to? Just stay close. I haven't ever tried this with anyone else before."

Twenty-One

A Hidden Home

Sir Rowan
  25th Day of the 1st Moon

Had I had any doubt in my mind before this day, certainly now
it would be banished.

The duel was inconsequential, save this: Lancelot's
knightlings cheat, and therefore it is no stretch to think
that Lancelot himself has sunk to unbecoming behavior.
Unfortunately I do not myself recall which of them it was
who struck me, but perhaps my lady could be called upon to
shed some light on the matter, if it becomes necessary. She
must have been very close by when it happened. Her testimony
would have to go through me to be acceptable in Knights' Court,
of course—but there is no point creating problems where we
have none, not yet. There are more important matters to note.

I believe, based on my observations at the time, that my injuries were indeed grievous. Fractured or broken ribs are to be expected from an unguarded lance hit, of course. But the sheer shock of the blow knocked me back against the saddle, causing bruising to the lower back, and a strain on my upper thigh which, given the speed with which the horses were traveling and the fact that my boot was caught in the stirrup, caused a break in my upper right thigh.

Note: is it possible the knightlings also tampered with my saddle? They knew the duel would be occurring. Perhaps this matter is more serious than I thought. Will examine saddle tomorrow.

Had Daisy not intervened when she did, I believe it likely that I could have died. I would have been very much at the mercy of the other knights.

The truly remarkable thing in all this is that now, as I write the events of the day, I am quite well. In fact I don't think I have felt better since my youthful days in the water clan's court. Whether that is due to the application of the bark of the Tree of Life or due to my lady herself, I could not say. I do not recall much of the procedure at all.

I *do* recall my lady's sweetness and concern when I came to, however, so well that I doubt there is any need for me to write it down. For as long as I live, I think I shall remember the sight of her face above mine.

As soon as she saw that I was well, she very prudently suggested I dress while she made some arrangements of her own. That was when I first recognized the state of my armor: some of the charms have been shattered, and the metal itself is dented in places, and a few of the clasps have broken. I will need to mend the mail and may as well replace the leg guard, which may indeed have been the real source of the tampering.

When she returned, my lady took my hand and led me to a darkened path of moss. I did not get a good look at the initial cavern we were in—the one which houses the Tree; but I did notice that everywhere the ground was soft and mossy, and there were these darkened patches scattered throughout. She tried to explain it to me, but I admit I was not fully focused at the time. It turned out that through some illusion magic, the darkened patches of moss actually serve as portals or hatches to a network of caverns below the first.

It is in this series of hidden caverns, then, that my lady resides. She led me through a number of them, each chamber connected by large tunnels of glittering rock, lit by glowing tendrils and roots descending from the ceilings. It was quite warm, and even cozy, despite a sense of disarray. My lady explained that often the pixies who visit her like to play tricks, making it difficult for her to maintain a sense of order. She does, however, maintain a variety of luxurious and truly impressive plants, which seem to thrive on that marvelous underground light. One large central chamber served as a sort of bedroom, she said—the sort of thing knightlings would refer to as a dragon's den, no doubt, though it seemed a perfectly enchanting place, with more soft mosses and a babbling spring. From this she retrieved a basket, and she began filling it with all kinds of flowers and mosses, mumbling to herself and moving about in almost clumsy haste. It warmed my heart to watch her; in fact, I didn't realize until too late that all I was doing was watching her, when I ought to have been helping.

"No, you shouldn't," she replied when I pointed this out. "I only brought you down here to keep you out of the pixies' way. I really think you ought to be resting. I just want to gather a few more things and then we can go to the tower—it isn't fixed yet, but it is quiet there, and you'll actually have a chance at sleep."

I will admit that, even though I had told her I felt fine, I had said so in my initial rush of gratitude and joy at finding her within arm's reach. Now that I was standing still, my head did ache, and my joints felt strangely tender, as though they'd been pulled apart and put back together. Which, of course, they had.

"Whatever you think is best, my lady," I said, meaning it fully, because it did seem to me that she had everything under control—far better than I might have hoped to do, were I in her position.

She paused and turned to me, flowers spilling from her basket. "Oh, I never seem to know what's best any more," she said, and though the truth of it struck me—it wasn't a joke—somehow in the next moment she smiled, and then we were both laughing. An effect of exposure to the Tree of Life, perhaps? In any case, she added, "Just as long as there aren't any more knights—and no more dragons either—then we should be just fine."

We looked at each other for the briefest of moments, and then again fell to laughing. The release I felt then must have borne me into some dreamland, for I remember only a haziness, and then a drowsy awareness that she carried me.

Twenty-Two

Knowing

Daisy

It really is a very strange thing to carry a knight. I hadn't noticed the first time, because I'd been so distraught. But carrying Rhys from the cave to the keep was harder—maybe because I was trying to carry along all his armor separately, since he hadn't put it back on, and at the same time trying not to wake him. It probably wasn't best to move him so soon, but I didn't feel quite at ease with him so near the pixies. For either one's sake.

Fortunately, the keep was still deserted—except for Nessie. I wasn't really surprised to find Rhys's horse there; Nessie is very smart, after all, and mostly I was just glad the other knights weren't around.

The landing woke Rhys up, and he helped me get things

settled. Nessie was quite happy in the stable, and I didn't even bother with the main hall—I took Rhys downstairs with me. He was still looking a little wobbly, so I convinced him to go lay down in my cot. I did my best to cover him up with lots of blankets—not really being sure exactly how many were needed, but figuring it was best to err on the side of too many—and then I went out into the kitchen. I got the main fire going, and then for a long time I simply sat there, staring at it.

I brought a stranger to the Tree, I was thinking.

Not only did I bring them there, I helped it heal them.

But Rhys isn't a stranger.

But I don't know him as well as I know the pixies.

But I feel right around him.

It felt right.

It felt like we were connected . . .

I could still hear Sha's words in my head. Sha is known to be the wisest of the pixies, in addition to the eldest. I love the pixies dearly, but it must be said that normally, to call someone the "wisest of the pixies" isn't actually saying very much. But Sha does have a sense for things, something that goes beyond knowing, and that's exactly what I was feeling right then. I felt kind of like a pixie myself, actually, very small and wavering and unknowing. But on the other hand, I didn't feel small at all—I felt more like myself than I have ever felt—strong, and bright, and joyful. I had saved Rhys, and everyone was alright.

Somehow, I realized, the actual detail of what happened—the letting someone in to see the Tree, something I thought I could never do—didn't matter half as much as the feelings involved.

Twenty-Three

Serving

Sir Rowan
  25th Day of the 1st Moon, cont.

My next cohesive memory is of waking in Daisy's room at the keep, under a veritable mountain of blankets. I hadn't even realized there were that many blankets in the entire tower. Excavating myself took a little time, but when at last I stood, I was pleased to note that my headache had receded and my stiffness had eased somewhat. However, I was ravenous as ever.

I emerged into the kitchen to find my lady tending the fire, throwing mosses on it which made the flames leap high and fill the room with warmth. She turned as soon as I opened the door, and when she saw me, the relief on her face was beautiful. I found it far more warming than the fire.

"If you're awake, you must be hungry," she said at once. "I'm so sorry—I don't often keep food in my home at the Tree, except as a treat sometimes, because those of us who live there are sustained by the Tree itself. I know you must need real food, though. I brought some herbs, but most of my garden didn't survive that storm. But there are things stored here, too, that the knights didn't take with them. Maybe we could make something of that?"

"I am certain we can, my lady," I agreed, and though my first impulse was to go to her and kiss her, I did my best to focus on practical matters. As I moved about the kitchen, she first pointed things out and then retreated to her habitual place along the counter, watching me carefully.

"Did you really mean it," she asked eventually, as I rummaged through storage bins and the basket of herbs she'd brought along, "that I can ask you anything? Because I can understand if there are things you don't want to say. But I really appreciate it, if you do."

At the time I found this shyness charming. I still find it so, but I think also it shows how deeply my lady feels her own inability to discuss matters freely with me. If only she knew how little it mattered, and could set her mind at ease!

Naturally I assured her that I had meant it, and so she began by asking, "Are you *certain* you're alright? Is there anything else we ought to do for you?"

"We are doing it now," I assured her, gesturing to the cold bread and herbs and scraps of cheese I had found. "If I have any other injuries, I have not noticed them."

She smiled, and admitted as I worked, "I have a weakness for the swiss at Lavender's. She always sends some up when people come. Alright then, I won't worry about that for now.

But what about later? Is it safe for you, out there? Why were the other knights attacking you like that?"

"It is much safer now that I know to be prepared," I said, and filled her in on the conflict between myself and Lancelot. She listened gravely, though she did also steal a rind of cheese from the cutting board.

"It was hard work carrying you around," she explained when I glanced at her, with a most becoming blush. Her pretty cheeks matched the color of her overalls, the same ones I had first seen her in.

"And I am eternally in your debt for the effort, my lady," I said. "How about grilled sandwiches?"

"Yes, please. And don't be silly," she said, answering both questions at once. "Why are the other knights so invested in this? I thought it was only your quest."

"It *was* my quest," I agreed, "and their interference has gone from presumptuous to indefensible. Naturally, I regret involving them in the first place. I had no idea how any of this would turn out."

"That I'd be the dragon, you mean?" she asked, her head at an angle.

"That they would go to such lengths, which are clearly uncalled for," I clarified. "It was *my* task, and mine alone, not set by any other. I can not explain their interest in it."

"I guess . . . if everyone thinks the Tree is so powerful, and that it's nearby . . . it's natural some people might want it," she said hesitantly.

"A quest is not meant to be simply a matter of wanting a new toy to play with or miracle to sell," I said, irritated not with her but with my former companions' behavior.

"What *is* a quest meant to be?" She looked at me as though

contemplating a question she'd never thought to ask before.

"A quest is a trial set specifically for the person involved. Or sometimes, it could be a way to atone." I hesitated, then cleared my throat. "In either case, it is a personal matter. Though others may help, they certainly can not take it over. Unless," I added, remembering Lancelot's comment about airs, "perhaps they believe I am not completing it in good faith."

"What does that mean?"

"It is possible," I said, "that they think I am working against the order of knights."

"As in, working for a dragon?" She caught her breath. "Like me?"

"They do not suspect you. I have been very careful about that," I said at once. "More likely they think I am 'rogue,' as the term goes. And to be truthful, they would not be so wrong in thinking so."

For several minutes Daisy was silent, watching me place our sandwiches on the grill above the fire. The more time passed, the more I knew I was right. Behind his insufferable bluster and insults, Lancelot certainly considered me a threat. There was even a chance, I realized, that he had been commissioned by the Knight's Court—or even by the clan. But I was not yet sure what to do about it.

At last, my lady said softly, "I think you are good, rogue or not. Can they not see that?"

"The Knights' Court is very . . . black and white," I told her. "It is one of the reasons I hesitate to consider myself one any more."

"You don't?" She didn't seem surprised, only probing. I answered her honestly.

"A knight serves someone, and I had all but given up service until I met you."

"Because of your past. Maybe you served your own sense of guilt," she said gently, watching me steadily. I thought then that her eyes were the same color as her wings, and nearly lost my concentration in thinking about them. It seemed to me I might never manage to cook her a meal without burning it. She went on, "You have been saying 'was' about your quest, haven't you? I only noticed it now."

"Yes, my lady. My reasons for seeking the Tree—" I hesitated. Did my reasons matter *more* now that I had found Daisy, or did they matter so much less? Even now, I am not certain. I know that they don't take up as much of my thoughts as they used to. And I know it is true, what I finally said: "In this instance your duty, my lady, is more important than mine."

"I—I see." She spoke very quietly, so I turned to face her. She added, "In that case, would you—would you mind not telling what has happened today to anyone else? Especially not the other knights."

"Of course," I promised at once. "In fact I will do better than that, my lady. I will send the other knights away, and tell them this quest is over. I was already attempting to do so when we fought."

"But Rhys," she protested, and as she said my name my reserve broke and I strode to her, "is confronting them again truly a good idea? Are you sure you could convince them without endangering yourself?"

"I will do it. I will make sure I am safe," I told her, placing my hand under her chin. "I will make sure they never come back again. On that you have my word."

She looked up at me, eyes shining, her lips parted as though to say some word of acceptance or thanks. Seeing this, how warmly she received my promise, I grew bold and sought to extract one from her in return. "My lady," I murmured, "may I ask something of you in the meantime?"

"Yes," she said softly. "What is it?"

"Please do not let it be days before I hear from you again," I whispered. "It has been agony, not knowing anything of you, not being able to see you or hear your voice."

Blushing, she said, "I didn't mean to—I didn't realize—I wasn't sure, you see, about how much I should say."

"Say anything you want," I told her. "Tell me as much or as little as you like. Only please do speak to me. Even if it is only to tell me about the weather."

"Oh, well, if that's all you're asking . . ." she smiled up at me, her lips so close to mine. "Very well."

She would have kissed me, I think, had we not at that very moment caught the scent of burning cheese.

Twenty-Four

The Outside World

⚘

Daisy

That night Rhys was very tired, and even though I kept thinking about what he'd said—*your duty is more important than mine*—I didn't want to press him about it. It seemed almost too good to be true, and I could have asked him so many questions. Instead, I made him a nest of blankets by the fire so that he could sleep warmly *without* being squished under layers of wool. And eventually, I laid down next to him and slept as well.

What a series of strange and magical things to relate! Unfortunately, the next morning, that strangeness took a turn for the worse.

It was Nessie who alerted us, actually. Rhys had slept in, and we'd only just finished a late breakfast when I heard Nessie calling, all the way from the stable. Rhys heard it too. And he realized what it meant before I did, and he started swearing.

Rhys ran upstairs—I think he meant for me to stay behind, but how could I have done that? I followed hard on his heels. We got to the main room just as the front door broke inward to reveal three of the other knights.

The older one, the kindly one, was gone. Instead, these were the three I had chased away from Rhys the day before. They didn't look at me at all—they didn't recognize me, of course. But they looked very menacingly at Rhys. And it didn't help that they had all their armor on, and he still just had a shirt and breeches and a cloak.

"I had a feeling we'd find you here," said the ringleader—Lancelot. He swaggered forward like he owned Lavender's keep.

"You had no right to come here," Rhys returned very coolly.

"Actually," said Lancelot, and the other two knights flanking him had their hands on their swords, "you might say it was our *duty* to track you down."

I couldn't help it—my temper flared. After all, I had just saved Rhys, and seen these knights cheating, and I was very tired of them picking fights. I didn't actually think—that happens when I get upset, unfortunately.

As though I wasn't completely unarmed and in human form, I stepped around Rhys at once. I stood right in front of him, staring Lancelot in the eye. I put my hands on my hips and stood up very tall—which would probably have worked better if I'd been my *actual* height—and I told them off:

"Who are *you* to talk about duty," I said, or something to that effect, "when all you have done is cause harm? First to that poor ice dragon, then to—to Sir Rowan, and even to Lavender. See what you've made of her kind hospitality! Sir Rowan asked for your help, and you responded by ganging up on him and trying to kill him. You've been nothing but bad luck this entire time. You ought to be ashamed of yourselves, but it's clear you never think of anyone beyond your own noses!"

Lancelot blinked at me. And then he laughed. So I did the one thing I know how to do in human form, which was to kick him squarely in the groin.

Well, he was wearing armor, so I'm not sure how much of it he actually felt. But he did fall back a few paces, and when he straightened up, he was angry. He paced back toward me with his eyes flashing. "You're getting too uppity for a cleaning lady," he said, "and you've been paying too much attention to our affairs. Been listening at keyholes, have you?"

He reached out as if to hit the side of my head, but I dodged out of the way. I would have kicked him again, but I'd forgotten about the other two knights. One of them caught me by the arm, and one fell back as Rhys hit them.

"You," said Lancelot, turning back to Rhys. "You're coming outside to talk things over with me, right now, civilized. I've got a proposition you're going to want to hear."

Rhys pulled back, frowning. "I'm not going anywhere."

"You are," Lancelot insisted, "unless you want to be responsible for her death." He looked at me, then again at Rhys. "*Another* death."

I had no idea what he was talking about, but clearly it was some secret between the two of them. Rhys seemed to understand completely. He promised me he'd be right back, but what good was that? I could see myself what the odds were. Lancelot, Rhys, and one of the extra knights went outside, while the other knight was still holding on to me in the hall.

Twenty-Five

A Defense

Sir Rowan
 26th Day of the 1st Moon, retrospectively

Note from Sir Rowan: I have added in this transcript to the best of my recollection afterward, because I did not record it in my journal at the time—I never had a chance.

Of course, I knew exactly what Sir Lancelot wanted to talk about. That is, I thought I did.

He pulled me out into the middle of the courtyard, sending Salna back a few paces. The world around us seemed impossibly bright, sun glinting off his armor, off the snowflakes in the air. The light itself was unfeeling.

"Let's stop beating around the bush," he said to me, his voice low and growling. "You might as well know by now why I *really* answered your call. You should have figured it out already—I was sent by the Grendales."

This shocked me, I must admit. I didn't say anything. I couldn't; there wasn't air in my lungs. I had expected him to say he was from the Court, and I was rogue, and on and on. Instead, here was a name from my past, tracking me down.

"Don't act surprised," said Lancelot impatiently. "You should have known there was a bounty on your head."

A *bounty*! But of course. "Then I was right, and you are no knight at all," I told him, sneering. "You're simply a mercenary. A headhunter."

"Ha!" Lancelot's laughter rang harshly, just as it had in the hall. "We *both* know that isn't true. Because they could just send anyone after the great Sir Rowan Grendale, could they? No one else would have made it back alive. No, they had to ask for the *best*."

"A generous way to refer to yourself, when all you've managed to accomplish is the destruction of a ruin and the angering of a dragon," I retorted.

"I'll tell you exactly what I've accomplished," Lancelot said, stepping in. "You're coming back to the Lake with me. They're going to put you on trial for everything you've done."

I stared at him. The surreal thing about it was that, had he come to me even a day before with that proposition, I might have agreed without even a need for violence. I knew, of course, that the trial would be merely the preliminary ceremony to an execution. The Grendales needed someone to blame, a scapegoat for the loss of their daughter and the scandal they'd endured. A previous version of myself might have agreed to be that scapegoat. I might have thought it was my duty; that it was exactly what I deserved.

But Daisy had given me new life, quite literally, and I found suddenly that I had no interest in returning to this old wound again and again. I turned away from Lancelot. I had nothing to say to him; I simply was prepared to walk away, back to where my lady was.

I should have known he would not let me do so, though. As I moved, he lashed out at me. The razor edge along the back of his metal glove sliced through my cloak and shirt, but his hand did not reach my skin. Instead, he came away holding a strip of bark.

I knew as soon as I saw it that I had made a terrible mistake.

Because I hadn't been able to leave it. Daisy had used that strip of bark from the Tree of Life to heal me, and when I'd found it amongst my clothes later, I'd kept it. I shouldn't have. There could be no lying about what it was. Its mossy surface glowed, even now, a day later. Lancelot knew what it was the moment he saw it, and I could say nothing.

"Salna!" he cried to his accomplice. "Go in there, and get that girl!"

Twenty-Six

A Secret Gone

Daisy

I waited for almost a full second after the doors closed behind Lancelot and Rhys before stomping on the feet of the knight who held me.

Actually, I thought that given the circumstances, that was pretty patient of me.

In any case, I don't know how long we were alone, but when the front door opened again, we were circling one another around a table, him brandishing a sword, me weilding a forgotten tankard I'd picked up. Of course we both looked to the light immediately—and my stomach plummeted when I saw it was one of the other knights. *Where's Rhys?* I wondered, when I probably should have been worried for myself.

The new knight hardly said a word—just rushed at me. So

then I had the two of them to worry about, and I could hear shouts and clanging from out in the yard, too. Nessie was making a racket again as well. Underneath it all, though, as I backed up against the wall and grabbed at a chair for cover, I managed to catch the briefest exchange between the knights—

"She's the one who's got the key to the Tree of Life," said one.

"Her? Really?" the other panted.

"They've got it outside as we speak! But they need *her* to make it work!"

Of course, much later, I realized that these knights were just full of nonsense, putting together pieces and coming up with strange theories. But I didn't know that at the time. Like I said, I tend to stop thinking when I'm upset. And even the briefest *idea* that these knights knew about the Tree or that Rhys had betrayed us somehow was enough to make me see red.

I screamed at them, I think, and that was when the trouble really began.

The thing is that even when I'm human, I still have some aspects of my true form, because the magic in my transformation necklace is just *magic,* after all, not a complete physical change in who I am. So there's things like me not feeling the cold, or still having some scales here and there, and—most importantly at that moment—still sometimes having *the voice.*

That's what my great-uncle used to call it. He never used it, and up until that moment, I never had either. My mother had once, on a band of robbers. We never saw them again.

I think most dragons in the rest of the world use this super-loud powerful call as a way to communicate over long distances, not to scare silly knights. (Although probably that too, if they get the chance.) And that might explain why, a few minutes later, I got that hum in my bones that told me we weren't alone.

The ice dragon had returned.

I didn't care at first. Somehow, I had turned the tables on the two knights, and had pushed *them* against the wall by the front door. I think I broke all Lavender's furniture. I hadn't transformed yet, but I was acting as though I had, because I just wasn't paying attention.

How could have been so stupid? I was thinking. *He's a knight—a knight with a duty!*

A duty, I feared, which could destroy us. He could be telling the whole world about the Tree. Even though he did not know where to find it or how to get through the pixies' charms—I *had* made him close his eyes as we left, at least—he could still do irreparable harm simply by calling attention to our existence. Not everyone he told would be blind, or foolish. Not everyone would focus only on the Tree.

There was no way I could leave the Tree or the pixies after that. There was no way, I thought, that I could ever face him again

Of course, none of those thoughts were actually relevant to the fight that was going on, which might explain the confusion.

In any case, shortly after I heard the ice dragon outside, there was a terrible yelp from outside—one of the knights—Lancelot. It was awful, the sort of sound that instantly tells you that something has died. It stopped me in my tracks long enough to realize I was still human, and this was bad. While I stood there, the other two knights ran outside. I followed them—but I made sure to transform as soon as I made it past the door.

The scene in the courtyard was just as bad as the scene inside. I spotted Rhys at once—he'd been hit by an initial icy blast from the ice dragon, I think, and lay off to one side, near the stable. The ice dragon itself had chosen to chase down Lancelot, who now was dead.

I'm not sure if it was touching, or foolish, but the two leftover knights were now charging the ice dragon. I roared at them, all three of them, trying to convince them to stop. It was no use, though. The ice dragon launched itself into the air and knocked another section of the wall down on top of its two attackers.

"You've had your revenge," I told it, launching myself into the air as well. "It is time to go home."

It looked at me so long I almost thought it wouldn't talk. Then it rumbled, "I sense magic here. I'll take what I'm owed." And then it dove for Rhys.

I dove too, of course. It sounds so haphazard, but this it how it always goes for me—I let instinct take over when I fight. I always thought it was because of my love for the pixies. I'm not sure why it would have worked so well for Rhys then, especially since I thought he might possibly have betrayed the Tree.

But it did work well, I must admit. The poor ice dragon couldn't even manage to fly away this time. He limped off quite miffed, and I knew he would find the nearest cave and stay there to recover. So I thought, as I hovered, watching him go, that I'd just tend to Rhys and Nessie and then go have a chat with the ice dragon, and then be home.

Simple.

Of course it didn't work that way. Nessie had run out of the stable and now was frozen straight through, and in no condition to carry Rhys anywhere. Rhys himself was alive but desperately cold, and he wouldn't wake up. There was no chance I'd take him back to the Tree again—but I also couldn't just leave him alone at a freezing stone tower, either. I had to make sure he got help.

So . . . that's how I ended up in the middle of Belville, wearing Rhys's cloak, standing over his body and yelling for help.

I'd had to fly in as myself, and then transform to get anyone to listen to me without running away. I didn't want to give myself away like that—not even Lavender had ever seen me, the real me. But I just couldn't think of anything else to do. Rhys was so cold, and getting colder all the time, and his shoulder was covered in blood.

I didn't know Belville well enough to know where to go, and I think most of the citizens of Belville probably didn't believe their own eyes. Fortunately, Red was one of the first people to come out. She took over right away, bringing me and Rhys into her shop, with her familiar William's help.

That's how we met, Red and me. She'd never even seen me before that—except in my true form, I think, maybe once or twice.

"It's alright," she kept telling me. "It's going to be just fine. You did the right thing."

With his magic, William—who looks like a nice fluffy dog, but must have very powerful magic, because he could lift Rhys and move him very easily, which is far more than the pixies could do—William brought Rhys upstairs, into the little apartment above Red's alchemy shop. There he laid Rhys out on the carpet in front of the fire, while Red tugged me up the stairs after her. I don't think my legs were working properly. Normally I am alright after transforming, just a little tired. But this time I couldn't stop shaking.

"William, you go and close the shop, then tell Officer Thorn what happened," Red directed. To me, she said, "I'm going to need your help with him. Can you do it?"

"Yes," I said, struggling a little to stay upright. "But I don't know how to heal. That's why I had to—I had to come here."

"Hmm. William, maybe grab Trent while you're out," Red called to her familiar. He was already bounding down the stairs.

Red had me help position Rhys, and then pass her potions and other tools from a medical kit on the floor. I sat there by his head and he never woke, and I kept thinking that somehow this, too, was my fault.

It wasn't until Red sat back and looked up at me that I realized I'd been crying.

"Come on," she told me, holding out her hand. "We've done all we can for now. He's going to be okay. Come over to the kitchen and have a cup of tea."

"Are you certain?" I asked, letting her lead me across the little apartment. As I leant on the kitchen island I could see Rhys by the fire, but he still seemed too far away, and too cold.

"I'm sure," said Red as she lit her stove and filled a kettle. "And we'll be even more sure when Trent gets here. There's no need to worry."

"I don't know Trent," I said, suddenly nervous. "I don't even know you."

"But you know Sir Rowan," Red pointed out, turning to look at me shrewdly as the water heated. "What was it you call him earlier?"

I hemmed and hawed, realizing that Rhys had given me his name in confidence, a confidence I didn't want to betray. Even if he *had* betrayed the Tree somehow.

"It's alright," Red decided. She looked amused as she watched me. "We'll just stick with the fact that you know him, and you two are friends. Fair enough?"

I nodded, a little unsure of what to say or even what I might say Rhys and I were.

Red nodded back and returned to her tea-making. "That's enough for now. He works here at the shop, did you know that? No? Well, it's only part-time. He's on leave right now, actually. But you can rest assured we have his best interest at heart, too."

Her hands hovered over two ceramic mugs. Her preparations reminded me of Rhys making dinner, and tending me.

He healed me, but I couldn't do anything for him, I thought rather desperately.

But I did do something for him, I reminded myself.

"I—I am glad you found us," I said. "Thank you."

"Don't worry about it." Red brought me a steaming mug, and leant next to me on the counter. "So, do you mind me asking who you are?"

I panicked and sloshed hot tea on myself. It didn't matter—it didn't burn me—but it was enough to make Red chuckle.

"Okay, how about a name at least?"

"You can call me Daisy," I said. Something about the mundane detail made me realize I needed to get back to my work, my duty. But it seemed too soon to leave.

"Hi Daisy, nice to meet you," Red said with a smile. "Can you tell me what happened? You don't have to talk about yourself."

I had just finished telling her about the ice dragon and the knights when footsteps pounded up the stairs.

"Aha!" said a very loud, greenish person in a uniform. "Tea break already? Where's your patient?"

"What do you need, Red?" A thin boy with purple streaks in his hair poked his head over the first person's shoulder. He seemed much more concerned.

"We got him cleaned up and stable for now. He's over there,"

Red told them, gesturing to the fire. "Trent, could you warm him up with a charm, maybe?"

"Don't tell me this was another attack like those ghosties at the castle," said the green person, coming over to us while Trent went to Rhys.

"No, sounds like this was an ice dragon, and unfortunately, three people are dead up on the mountain. You'll have to go and check that out—but it sounds like there's nothing to be done right now. Oh, Daisy, this is Officer Thorn," said Red. I glanced back at the officer and nodded politely. But I'd been watching Trent while they spoke. He waved glowing hands over Rhys, who was still sleeping. Trent, I realized, must be a Witch. I'd never met one, and he seemed very young, but it made sense why Red would want his help.

"And you, if stories are to be believed, are also a dragon," Officer Thorn said. It took me a moment to realize she was speaking to me.

"I—I don't—um—" I hesitated, unsure what to say. Finally I burst, "I work for Lavender."

Officer Thorn looked me over. Despite her brash manner, her gaze was not unlike Red's. *These are nice people,* I thought. I felt badly for not telling them more, but I didn't feel that I could.

"Up at the keep on the mountain, where this all went down," said Officer Thorn at last. "'Sat right? I always wondered who she could've found to watch over that godsforsaken place."

"It grows on you," I protested.

"'Sat right?" Officer Thorn said again. Then she threw back her head and laughed.

"Ignore her, Daisy," said Red with a groan. "She likes puns. It's annoying. Where's William?"

"Tending to the small army of gossips standing outside your door," said Thorn. "It's not every day you see a dragon saving a knight, now, is it?"

Once again she looked at me, but this time her smile was so endearing I almost found myself smiling back.

"Did I?" I asked them, glancing at Trent again. "Did I save him? Are you *sure* he'll be alright?"

"Trent, you answer," Red called across the room. "She didn't believe me the first dozen times I said it."

"Sir Rowan's going to be fine," Trent announced as he bounced up on his feet. He pushed his hair back from his face as he looked at me. "I'm guessing it was a laceration on the shoulder, several broken ribs, and the ice spell, right?"

"Right," Red answered, "as far as I could tell. But what do you mean it *was* several broken ribs? I couldn't fix those."

"I think I did," Trent beamed. "I've been working on my healing."

I bit my lip. "You *think* you did?"

"Don't you worry," Thorn assured me. "Trent talks unprofessional, but he's good at his work. Sir Rowan'll be right as rain."

"Look who's talking," Trent said amiably. He stepped over Rhys and came over to join us in the kitchen. "Got any cookies, Red? I'm starving. William made us think it was a deathly emergency."

"It *was* an emergency," I said, baffled.

Red and the others exchanged a smile that I didn't understand. "William's fan club might have an unexpected member," she remarked to them. To me, she said, "Daisy, you're right, of course. But we look after each other here. Everything's going to be fine now. And that's thanks to *you*. So you can relax now—I'm sure you've had a really hard day too."

She looked at me rather knowingly as she said it, and I realized suddenly that I was still wearing nothing but my necklaces and Rhys's cloak, which had fallen off of him when we were flying. I'd caught it thinking I'd put it back on him. Somehow, none of my plans for the day had worked out.

"I—I'll be back," I promised, setting down my tea. "I have to go and—check some things."

"Want company?" Officer Thorn asked. She, too, looked knowing. "Or would I only slow you down?"

"I appreciate it, Officer," I stammered. "But I'll be okay. I'll be—I'll be right back." I hurried to the door, only pausing to say, "Thank you—all of you. Thank you for looking after him."

Twenty-Seven

Another Life

Sir Rowan
  28th Day of the 1st Moon

I had the strangest dream. I was at work—or at least, I was in Red's Alchemy and Potions, perhaps in the back room. I had a feeling as though I was laid out on a table, like the cursed princess in some strange retelling of Snow White. I tried to move, but my body seemed so slow and far away. But I could see shapes moving beyond me—at first I thought they were dwarves; then one came out of the crowd, and suddenly it was night and there were stars behind her, and she was wearing some pink robe that fell over me as she leaned forward. Her lips brushed my forehead, and she gave me a command: "you must recover. You must."

I do not usually remember my dreams. On the whole, I

place no stock in divination or projections. And yet now as I wake, this one stays with me, lingering at the edges of my consciousness.

Perhaps it is because I am not yet stable. I saw Red earlier this morning, and I believe I can piece together exactly what happened. It is the concussion which is still affecting me, no doubt. My shoulder aches but is healing apace, and thanks to the young Witch, I do not feel cold at all.

I remember clearly the confrontation with Lancelot, and talking about the Grendales, and the Tree; but that is where I become confused. I can see so clearly the Grendale matriarch, talking about the Tree of Life and how it should have been hers—but that conversation was centuries ago, wasn't it? Never before have I felt this particular downside of longevity: all my life seems to be running together. Most distressingly, I can't recall what happened to Daisy or where Nessie is. As soon as I am free from here, I may have to prepare the ingredients to resummon its physical form.

If I were a healer of any sort, I would be convinced to set up shop in Belville after this experience. I am not in Miss Red's shop, thank goodness, but I *am* in her apartment (perhaps the lingering smells and noise from downstairs pervaded my dreams?). Sleeping on a couch hardly seems like an appropriate way to recover, but I take it they feared to move me to the tavern, worrying that the outside cold would cause a relapse in my condition. Had I been awake, I could have pointed out to them that the only thing that can cause a relapse into an ice blast is an *ice dragon*. Apparently, none but I have seen it near town. I can only think . . .

. . . But I have not wanted to think it.

Perhaps I had better write the entire conversation down.

I first woke very early this morning, and then again regained consciousness as Miss Red was making breakfast. It was the smell of raspberry muffins and cheesy eggs which convinced me to wake, I think. Miss Red is an admirable cook.

As I am on the sofa, however, she could not see me from the kitchen. Instead it was William sitting in his window seat who noticed me wake. I believe he may have been keeping watch.

"You're awake! You're awake. I *told* her," he said at first, then shouted across the house at Miss Red, "I told you to make something good for Sir Rowan. He's awake!"

"Heard you the first time," Miss Red called back. "How are you feeling, Sir Rowan?"

I had to clear my throat several times before I could speak. "Remarkably better than I might have expected," I managed to say at last. I could not quite sit upright, as my shoulder seemed likely to split and my head pounded when I moved.

"You're lucky—" Miss Red began to say.

But William interrupted her, his tail thumping against the wooden window frame around him. "You were *rescued*. Why didn't you tell us you knew the dragon?"

"Which dragon?" I asked, confused and even in my state, hesitant to identify Daisy as such.

"*William*," Miss Red reprimanded from behind us. "Don't you dare—"

"She said her name's Daisy," said William. "Is that true? Seems like a strange name for a gigantic dragon guarding the Tree of Life."

"*William!*" This time Miss Red's voice was so loud and pointed that William could ignore her no longer. He put his ears back and managed to look slightly abashed as Miss Red continued, "She practically begged us not to tell anyone she'd been here. Have you been spreading rumors all over town?"

"She started it herself," William mumbled resentfully. "*She's* the one who flew into town and even brought you a special tea. It *glows.* After everything Sir Rowan told those knights, how could we *not* realize it's from the Tree of Life? What does she think we are, idiots?"

"No, but she *did* think she could try to trust us," Miss Red retorted.

I had a feeling I'd woken from unconsciousness into a very bad dream—or a horrible alternate reality. In the silence, I finally managed to say, "Excuse me. Are you saying that Miss Daisy came here, but she didn't want me to know? And—that *everyone* in town knows what I said to Sir Lancelot now?"

"Yes," said William.

"Now, stay calm," said Miss Red, more diplomatically. It wasn't until she came over from the kitchen and laid one oven-mitted hand on my good shoulder that I realized I'd struggled halfway upright.

"She flew right into the Square," William continued. "Also, Sir Lancelot's dead."

Above me, Miss Red spoke sharply. "William, go to the kitchen and make tea. Keep an eye on the muffins, they're almost done. I don't want to hear anything more from you except 'breakfast is ready.'"

In my time with Miss Red and William, I have only seen her speak like this twice. Each time it is undeniably effective. William slunk away from the small living area and remained silent.

Miss Red, meanwhile, seated herself on an ottoman near the sofa. Her manner softened a great deal, but I think that only pained me more.

"I think we're just going to have to start from the beginning," she said quietly. "You have to understand, no one was trying to deceive you. I was *hoping* we could protect Daisy, is all. The same way she wanted to protect you."

The words were blades in my heart.

"Daisy's the one who brought you here," Miss Red continued. "That was two days ago. The other knights all fell while fighting the ice dragon, it sounds like. She told me what had happened to you and helped me and Trent heal you. Later, she came back with tea, just like William said. I'm making it for you now. But she asked us to keep her role in the whole affair a secret. And yes—that includes from you. I thought it was strange, I'll admit, but you have to understand, she was very upset by everything that had happened."

"She revealed herself," I realized, the mounting chagrin of it all making me wish I'd never woken up.

"Yeah. Right in Market Square, as William said. I don't think she had any other choice," Miss Red added gently. "She wanted to do everything she could to save you. It's just too bad," she added more loudly, for William's benefit, "that everyone can't focus on *that* and instead feel the need to gossip about *her.*"

"Everyone knows it?" I whispered.

Miss Red eyed me. "Well, 'knows' is a strong word. Officer Thorn has her theories, of course."

The mention of the Officer sent a chill down my spine. "She wouldn't—"

"No. No one has any reason to harm Daisy. Isn't that right?" Miss Red asked, again looking toward the kitchen.

"Everyone at Lavender's says the ice thing is a big cover, and she's the Guardian of the Tree of Life and Sir Rowan found it so she kicked him down the mountain—and then she felt bad and brought him here. Or maybe she planned for him to die here instead of up there," William said, over sounds of shuffling and pouring. "Breakfast is ready."

"That's ridiculous," I protested.

"Either way, the fact is you're both alive and well," Miss Red told me. "And if you want to be *really* well, then I suggest you eat and drink."

Twenty-Eight

Making A Deal

Sir Rowan
29th Day of the 1st Moon

I left off very early yesterday, and have much to relate now. The truth is though that I accomplished little yesterday at all. I did not take either of Miss Red's suggestions. I was, I am ashamed to say, mired in my own sense of guilt over the entire affair, and terribly pained by thinking constantly of how Daisy must think of me.

It took me until this morning to finally think of how Mme Lavender must be thinking of *her*.

When at last I realized what a terrible position my silence placed Daisy in, I immediately got up. I asked Miss Red to make Daisy's tea for me again, and thankfully, there was just enough left that she could. It was, as William had suggested, tea from the Tree of Life. While not as potent as direct application of the bark, it had a warming and invigorating effect from the inside out. Pained only by my shoulder and my own stupidity, I left Miss Red's very early this morning to seek out Mme Lavender.

I arrived too late. But only just.

Mme Lavender was in her office, which is a small room set in the back corner of the tavern, entered through the kitchen. She is never in it normally. But when I didn't see her at the bar, I knew where to go. I made my way directly through the kitchen, not pausing to explain myself, and when I found that the door was ajar I pushed my way in.

"You'll have to understand, I just can't do it," Mme Lavender was saying.

"But you must understand that I *didn't* do anything," said another, much dearer voice. As I strode in, I very nearly collided with Daisy.

She was in her human form, naturally, in a yellow sweater and high boots. And she was distraught.

I wanted to hold her, to steady us both, but I recollected at the last minute that she wouldn't be pleased at all to see me. After all, I was the one who had given away her secrets and caused all this trouble for her. I turned at once to face Mme Lavender behind her desk.

"She didn't do anything," I echoed, less forcefully than I'd hoped. "Nothing except save my life."

"Sir Rowan." Mme Lavender nodded graciously at me, perhaps glad of a distraction. "I'm very glad to see you up and about, lad. And your word means a great deal to me, as always. But it isn't *me* I'm worried about. As I was just explaining to Daisy, I have the thoughts and fears of the town to think of. I can't run an outpost on the mountain right now—much less run one managed by someone of questionable standing, where people have *died*."

"I know what they are saying," I said, thinking of William's report yesterday. "But not a word of it is true. The knights turned on me, and our fight drew the attention of the dragon. Miss Daisy *saved* me," I insisted.

Mme Lavender looked between myself and Miss Daisy, who stood just out of arm's reach beside me. "And it *is* the same ice dragon which has now attacked my keep twice, I take it?"

The both of us affirmed this, myself emphatically, Daisy reluctantly.

Mme Lavender looked at me. "Did you kill this dragon?"

"No," I answered honestly, "I was caught unawares and would certainly have died, had not Miss Daisy come along."

Mme Lavender looked now to Daisy. "And did *you* kill the dragon?"

Daisy paused, then shook her head. My poor lady! I think she was very uncomfortable talking about her actions as a dragon to her employer. And she never would have needed to, had it not been for me! "I—I bested him, but I didn't kill him," she said very quietly. This was news to me, because of course no one in town knew it; but it didn't surprise me at all. "I only wanted him to leave, so I could get—could get Sir Rowan. I thought I would go back later and talk him into leaving the mountain. But I—I never did."

"Why didn't you?" Mme Lavender asked.

When Daisy hesitated again, I stepped forward. "Must you ask? Is it not enough to know that Miss Daisy did not attack me?"

"This is my business," Mme Lavender said to me with a piercing gaze. "And my business involves peoples' lives. So yes,

I must ask."

Understanding no doubt that her job was at risk, Daisy cleared her throat. "I was very busy—and upset. After I left Sir Rowan with the alchemist, I had to check on—my home. And then I went back to Red with things for Sir Rowan. And then I—I just wasn't thinking straight."

Mme Lavender settled back in her chair and regarded the two of us contemplatively. Sensing that she was hesitant to reopen her keep (and thus have cause to re-employ Daisy) if the deaths went unresolved and an ice dragon remained on the loose, I said impetuously, "*I* will go and find the dragon. If I can not convince it to leave, I will slay it and bring you the proof. Will that be enough?"

Mme' Lavender's gaze turned shrewd. "What makes you think you can kill it now if you didn't before?"

"I will be more prepared," I began, when to my surprise, my lady interrupted.

"*I* will go," she said. "It is my fault anyway; I left it undone."

"My lady," I protested, forgetting myself and our where-abouts, "you shouldn't have to face such a foe alone."

"But it's my *job,* alone," she returned. For the first time she looked me full in the face. I knew she wasn't talking about any responsibility she had to Mme Lavender, but instead was thinking of the Tree. The fierceness glinting in her eyes took my breath away.

"You both go," Mme Lavender broke in. "Those are my terms. I want you both to go and handle this, and make sure to bring back proof when you're done. Not just for me—for the entire town. Do you understand?"

My lady sidled, and I hesitated. "But—"

"No buts," Mme Lavender insisted. "You both go. I'm hedging

my bets, you see. Now, do we have a deal or not?"

I looked to Daisy, who looked to Mme Lavender. "My job at the keep—"

"We'll talk about it again when this is over," Mme Lavender said, not unkindly. "Deal with this first, and then I'll listen. Yes?"

Reluctantly, Daisy nodded. Seeing this, I too acquiesced.

I have arrangements to meet Daisy outside of town in just a few moments—just after the stroke of ten in the morning, we said. She was very uncertain and kept her gaze downcast. It is no surprise! I can't make a mess of this. I had better collect my things—

Twenty-Nine

The Hunt

Daisy

Since there's no chance at all that my brother will read this far, I may as well come about and say it. I was confused and mad at Rhys when the knights first talked about the Tree, it's true. But everything shifted when I found him in peril. I didn't understand myself until I was back at home, and he was at Red's, healing. My heart hurt constantly, thinking of him. I even dreamed about him, when I finally did manage to fall asleep.

The thing about the Tree of Life is that it's meant to support and inspire *life*. Aside from creating a safe haven, the whole point of it is that life itself is valuable.

And Rhys's life, it turned out, was especially valuable to me.

I could tell, when we met outside Belville to go up the

mountain once more, that he thought I must be angry at him. He was wearing that invisible mantle of guilt over his shoulders. The truth was, my entire body felt light just seeing him and knowing that he was okay. But I didn't tell him that—I didn't tell him I wasn't angry, that what was done was done. I thought it best that I keep my distance somehow, anyhow. I thought if I got too close to him that I'd make another mistake.

And since we were going to find a very violent dragon, any mistake might cost another life.

"I'm afraid I haven't located Nessie," he said as we stood awkwardly in the forest.

"Nessie was frozen," I told him. "I can show you where."

He took a deep breath. "I would be indebted to you, my lady."

I hesitated, feeling very sorry for him. "Can you—can anything be done?"

"Yes, I should be able to perform a resummoning spell," he said with a slow nod. "But in the meantime, I fear I will slow you down."

"No, you won't," I said. I had already thought this through, as I waited for him to get ready. "I think it's best if I go as myself, and you ride on my back."

A light flashed in his eyes, a brief moment of hope. I watched it, biting my lip. Quickly it was gone, and he agreed to my plan.

We flew silently over the forest, climbing higher through the clouds, paralleling the moutain's ascent. It occurred to me after a time that Rhys probably wouldn't speak until I spoke to him. After all, he rarely did anything before I indicated that it was alright.

Part of me wanted to ask him why the same hadn't applied to the Tree. Why had he told Sir Lancelot about it, and about me?

But I already knew the answer. I had figured it out the day before. It was the only answer that made sense, given that the knights had all continued fighting until the ice dragon showed up. Rhys had told Lancelot because he was forced to, or because he was trying to get rid of the knights—as he'd promised to do.

"I have a good idea where he's gone," I said eventually, meaning the ice dragon. "We can start there."

Rhys shifted, leaning along my neck. He had to shout against the wind. I would have heard him even if he spoke normally—I have very good ears—but I thought the effort was endearing.

"My lady," he said, "how do you think it best we approach him?"

"We may as well face him together," I said, after thinking a moment. "He knows I was fighting to save you. If we stand together, there's a better chance he'll listen than if it was just one of us."

"And if he does not listen at all?"

"He's still injured," I pointed out. "I doubt he has had the benefit of healers. He'd have to be truly magic-tinged to wish to fight in his condition."

The term was unfamiliar to Rhys, and I had to explain it. Once I did, he said, "Do you think the effects of the summoning spell have lasted so long?"

"I wondered that too," I admitted. "I think it isn't the spell exactly, but maybe his lingering anger about the spell that's made him irrational."

"Is there any way to return him to wherever the knights summoned him from?" Rhys asked after a moment's consideration.

I hadn't thought of that. "I don't know—I'm not good with magic. Can you think of any way?"

"I admit I am not proficient with magic either, my lady."

"In that case," said I, beginning my descent, "we'll have to hope that talking to him works."

I knew the ice dragon couldn't have gone far from the keep, but it still took all morning to find him. I flew low over the trees while we kept a lookout for broken trunks or other signs of a dragon passing by. At one point I considered taking a break so that Rhys could get Nessie—in fact I offered to do so—but he said he had to wait until a full moon. So we continued our flight around the mountain, and just as afternoon began to wane, we found a promising cave.

I landed gently, and Rhys hopped down at once. The cave was more a chasm between two rocks, surrounded by trees, which the ice dragon had crushed underfoot. I was unfamiliar with the terrain and didn't want to get too close. The ice dragon was much larger than me, after all, and might have an advantage in close quarters. Besides, I doubted Rhys's vision in the dark—and in caves, therefore—was very good.

"We come in peace," I called out in a formal draconic greeting. "We wish to discuss your presence on the mountain."

Rhys and I waited for a long moment.

Finally there was a rumble, and a laugh. "Who is this 'we'?"

The ice dragon's voice was as cold and harsh as a winter wind. Looking down at Rhys, I saw that he too could understand the words. *Good,* I thought.

"Sir Rowan Grendale of the Tipped Ewer," Rhys introduced himself.

"Shining Gift of Earth and Light, Guardian of Gold-tree," I said, giving the literal translation of the title my mother had given me rather than the nickname I used with my friends. "And what may we call you?"

But rather than answer politely, the ice dragon laughed

again. There was a labored scraping and shuffling, and after a moment—after Rhys and I had promptly backed up—the ice dragon's great blue head appeared in the gloom at the entrance of the cave.

"I'll have no dealing with you," he said, looking between us. "I'll have nothing to do with a dragon who consorts with humans!"

"But neither of us have intended you any harm," I protested. "The ones who summoned you are long gone, by your own claw. It does no one any good—"

"I *said*," bellowed the dragon, "I will not stand to be lectured by an unnatural filthy whore!"

I was shocked into silence. No one, in my long life, has *ever* spoken to me that way.

There was a *fwing* and a flash beside me as Rhys drew his sword. "We came with civil terms," he said, "but we are just as prepared to meet your incivility."

The ice dragon took one look at Rhys and yanked his head back. A moment later, ice filled up the chasm between the rocks.

Rhys muttered a word which Red has since informed me should *not* be repeated.

When the ice dragon stayed gone, and I remained silent, Rhys looked up at me. "My lady? What shall we do?"

"I—I don't know," I said, more in shock than anything else. I had always known that my connection to Rhys might be considered unusual, of course. But the vitriol of the ice dragon still surprised me. *Why should he care?* I couldn't help but think. "I suppose we'll have to break in, or lure him out somehow."

"He'll have to come out eventually," Rhys said. Grimly, he settled in to wait.

I crouched beside him, though I remained quiet. *How could he have known?* I kept wondering. *Just because I save someone doesn't mean I am a traitor to my kind. And just because—just because—I like someone who is different—Why should it matter?* That is the thought I kept coming back to. And I was angry—very angry, at the ice dragon, for making it matter. I had half a mind to break into his stupid cave and tell him exactly what I thought of his backwards ways.

But others would think the same way, I knew. And what would other dragons think, if I were to slay one of my own kind on account of some strange humans?

My family has always been on the outside, but at least we have never been targets of disdain and distrust before.

Now I understood what Rhys meant about the other knights being suspicious of him.

But by the time I had thought all this through, and restrained myself a good many times from leaping up to fight or taking to the wing to leave all this behind, the sun was setting.

"I brought extra provisions," Rhys was saying. It took me a while to realize that he was talking to me, and that so much time had passed.

"We can't stay out here in the clearing," I protested. "You will freeze."

Rhys's mouth opened and shut. Finally he said, "I can make myself a shelter if you wish to stay. It seems unwise to retreat all the way back to the village."

"The keep isn't far from here," I said, without a second thought. "We could stay there. Lavender said that Officer Thorn and some others went and cleaned it up and retrieved the knights. Even though the walls aren't fixed, the kitchen is still fine."

"Perfect," Rhys agreed.

I considered piling trees up in front of the chasm or shouting insults before we left, but decided better of it. The ice dragon was going nowhere. He would stay in that hole, bitter and angry, for as long as he could—that much I knew. We could make a plan and come back tomorrow.

Thirty

Duty and Lies

⁓⦿⦿⁓

Sir Rowan
  29th Day of the 1st Moon, cont.

I am back at the keep, and it is very, very late; the fire in the hearth is mostly embers now. But I must write before I fall asleep, lest I forget anything.

There is nothing to note about the ice dragon, save that it is repugnant and it made Daisy very upset. When we finally came back here and I made my way to the kitchen to begin dinner preparations, it took her a long while to comport herself and join me.

I admit, a part of me feared she *wouldn't* join me. She had been so silent and strange, all day long. When at last she came and sat at the kitchen table in her pale green leggings and lavender tunic, every fiber of my being seemed to sigh. I hadn't even realized I'd been holding my breath.

"Dinner will be a stew," I said, endeavoring to keep my voice even. "You'll have to forgive the quality, as it is from a dried mix."

"It's alright, Rhys," she said softly. The quality of her voice was enough to make me think she wasn't talking simply about the soup. I rose from the hearth and went to sit beside her on the bench.

"My lady," I asked, once I had summoned the courage to do so, "how can it be alright, after the way that dragon mistreated you? And everything that has happened in town? All products of my own single-mindedness. I assure you, I never meant—"

"It's alright," she repeated more emphatically, glancing my way with a very small smile.

"Please, allow me to apologize," I begged her. The urge had been growing within me all day, and at that moment I felt I might perish on the spot if she continued to think poorly of me, and if this too would be added to the list of deeds for which I could not atone.

"What good does it do," she asked, without looking my way, "to go over and over painful things?"

"I do not want you to be in pain," I said promptly. "Let me carry the burden instead; it was my mistakes that brought us here. Please, my lady, if you will not let me explain, then be angry at me—let me know what you think of me. I am certain I deserve it."

At that, she turned, and her gaze met mine. Very steadily she said, "You don't deserve to be ranted at, Rhys."

"I do," I insisted.

"You don't. Not now."

"I do. I forced you out of retirement and endangered myself

in foolhardy battles, not once but twice. I was unconscious and therefore absent when you most needed someone to support you. And I sold your secrets for the price of my own sentimentality!"

"I'm not mad that you were unconscious," she protested. Then, looking at me from the corner of her eye, she asked, "That bark Sir Lancelot had—it *was* what we used to heal you. Why did he have it?"

"I picked it up first for sentimental reasons," I repeated, modesty preventing me from speaking the absolute truth in the matter. "I never would have given it to him. But when I turned to leave him, he reached out and happened to take it from my person. I didn't mean for it to happen, but if I had only thought—"

"I tell you, it's alright, Rhys," she interrupted once more. "You didn't know."

For a moment there was only the sound of the crackling fire and the wind rushing around the keep above.

"I know that you guard the Tree and have kept it secret these long years, and now I have exposed you—and it—to innumerable questers and entrepreneurs," I said at last.

"That's not quite right." My lady turned and again looked at me with a slight, wry smile on her face. "Rhys, you heard me earlier when I introduced myself."

That I had. Both dragons had spoken the common language for me, and I had remarked upon her name—her *full* name, just as long and symbolic as I have always heard rumor that dragon names are. Shining Gift of Earth and Light, Guardian of Gold-tree. I didn't understand it at the time, but there were so many other matters to attend to that I didn't ponder it at all. And besides, who was I to complain that my lady had given me a nickname rather than her full title?

"Ask me what my duty is," she said, her voice a whisper.

But even as I formed the words, I began to understand. She watched me as I stumbled over the phrase. Her smile grew.

"I thought you should know," she told me. "It seems only fair. And maybe—maybe it explains things. You see, the story you were told is true. And it *does* have to do with the Tree. But the Tree was planted to be a safe haven for pixies who feared persecution from their neighbors in Belville. It was a way for them to grow beyond their troubles. That's what—that's what the Elders always tells me. You would know them as the priestess, and the hermit, and Gold-tree."

I stared at her, ashamed. "I—I had no idea . . ."

"I know." She nodded, and gently—almost timidly—placed her hand over mine. "I didn't want to tell you. I wasn't sure if I could, even though Gold-tree herself told me I ought to. But that's why it matters—not because of the Tree itself. Because of what might happen to the pixies if they're found."

"Saints forgive me," I murmured. "My lady, I didn't know—apparently, everyone in town has heard—they may have already—"

"Yes. But it's alright so far. I check on them whenever I can. Would you like to see?" She drew closer to me, pulling her locket from beneath her neckline as she did so, and looping its long chain around my neck. She opened the locket and for a moment it glowed, a bright golden hue, before the spell completed and through the interior of the locket a little picture of the Tree of Life could be seen, with colored light swirling around it. My lady's cheek brushed mine as she smiled. "Can you see them, flying around? I told them to do that. I told them to keep patrols. I didn't mean they should do it so *quickly*, but at least they are on their guard."

"Then you are their . . ." My voice trailed off; it was very difficult to think, not only because of this revelation, but because I could smell the herbal perfume of her hair, and I could feel the warmth of her body along mine. I had thought she might never come so close to me again.

"Guardian," she finished for me. "The Tree is their sanctuary, and I am their guard. My family has held that duty for generations."

"I didn't tell anyone *where* I'd got the bark from," I said impulsively. "Not Lancelot, and not anyone in town. I never gave any kind of direction. And I didn't say anything actually about you or the pixies. Although everyone has pieced that together—about you at least."

"Yes, so they have." My lady closed the locket and let it drop, but she did not move away. Instead she shifted so her head hung at an angle to mine, close enough that I could feel her breath, which wavered—as though she was undecided about something. Anxious. I myself was afraid to move, lest my trembling hands betray me. "It feels good to tell you," she said, very softly, almost as though she was speaking to herself. "All this time I have been worried about how much to say. But to say everything—it feels good. Rhys . . . Sha, the priestess, she says we are connected. I don't understand why, but I feel it. But together, we attract a certain kind of danger—a kind of suspicion . . ."

I clutched at her hand, still laid over mine. "You feel connected to me?"

"I can't explain it," she said ruefully. "But it turns out I'm not much good at denying it, either. You should have seen the way Red and the Officer looked at me . . ."

I didn't care one whit for Officer Thorn or Miss Red at that particular moment. I turned to put my arm around her, to draw her in and kiss her, but paused at the last moment, our noses brushing. "Do you wish to deny it, my lady?"

"It's not fair to ask me that now," she murmured, though her hand on my collar didn't permit me to back away or give her space. "There are so many reasons we ought to."

"I don't care about any of them."

"I don't remember why I did, either," she said, her lips teasing mine. "Except the pixies. But if you would distract me from them when you're away, then perhaps I ought to keep you close . . ."

"I will help you keep them safe," I said at once. "I swear it."

Even as I spoke, she pulled me into her. My words were lost against her mouth. She kissed me passionately, as though I'd been lost to her forever and returned by a miracle—and so I suppose I had been, twice over: but the miracle was of her own doing. Fully aware of this, I embraced her eagerly and surrendered myself to her warmth. *Let love heat the long winter nights,* as the old saying goes.

She kissed my cheeks, the tip of my nose, and my forehead, as though she was knighting me all over again. I like to think of it that way, though knowing her ignorance regarding knights, I doubt she meant the gesture as such. Nevertheless I smiled, thinking these thoughts, and caressed her hair as she paused for breath.

"I have missed you," I confessed then. "Even though I was certain you'd never want to speak to me, I couldn't stop thinking of you."

My lady smiled, tilting her head at me. "I'm not so unreasonable that I can't speak to people who have made me upset."

"What about kissing them?"

Her smile grew. "Is that the real reason you went to find Lavender, and agreed to seek out the ice dragon?"

"Not quite," I said, "but it is reason enough."

Not long after, a bubbling pot reminded me that—once again—I had neglected dinner. My lady freed me from the locket chain and we ate our soup nestled close together, watching the fire. We resolved to talk of the ice dragon in the morning. Instead, I told her everything Red and William had told me, and she blushed and laughed as she recounted her meeting with everyone upon delivering me to town.

"I don't care if they know who I am," she said when I worried once more about her transformation in the Square. "Not for my sake. I'm only worried about giving away the pixies' secret."

"It can hardly be secret if the other pixies were involved, and are still aware of the story," I pointed out cautiously. By that time, I was rinsing out dishes in the sink.

"Maybe not in the strictest sense," my lady agreed, though she remained at the table. Too far away. "But it is—different, dealing with pixies. They live such long lives, and yet they only ever think of the present. They know things, and then they forget them. And then, if they are reminded, suddenly they become interested again all in a rush . . ."

"I see," I said, understanding at last. "You worry about causing renewed interest from the pixies in Belville."

"Silver-Tree," said Daisy absently. "My pixies almost never speak of her, or of anyone else beyond their home. They've become two completely separate groups."

This seemed to be the cause of the tension that ruled my lady's life. I at once set to thinking about it, though admittedly I still know very little of pixies. "Forgive me, my lady, but if the one group of pixies *did* descend upon the other, what would you be called to do?"

"You mean, why fight tiny creatures with a massive dragon?" She was smiling; I turned as I dried the dishes, in order to watch her face. "My family is there in part because pixies love to exaggerate. They wished for the thing that seemed like the very last word in protection, and so they got my great-great-grandfather. Also I think it is in part because of the Tree. It is expected, when you have a Tree of Life, to have a very impressive guardian. I *would* fight on their behalf, of course, especially if the other pixies summoned something scary. But ultimately I don't have any idea what that fight would look like, and that's why it unnerves me."

In this, my lady told me a great deal more than she expected to. I was not terribly surprised to learn that there could be more than one Tree of Life; in fact that makes sense, given my own experience. I recall that the water fairies of Grendale often spoke of *Trees* of Life; I had thought this merely a misconception, especially because the clan had claim to no magical trees to speak of. Despite their pretentions in the matter, of course. They thought they were owed everything; I should I known I would not be able to escape them unscathed.

It is also interesting to me upon reflection that, despite her undeniable prowess in battle, my lady worries about what she might be called upon to do. And it speaks very well of her that for her charges, she would face the unknowable so matter-of-factly.

But what particularly stood out to me at the time was the question of my lady's heritage. I stopped drying the ladle and stood looking at her dumbly for a moment before she asked me what was on my mind.

"Do you mean to say, my lady," I asked her, "that your ancestor was born of a wish?"

She smiled once more. "One story I heard says that Gold-Tree, at her mother's hands, had nearly died three times. And so, the pixies' deity saw fit to grant her three gifts. Three gifts of life," she explained softly, "for three untimely deaths. One was the cave they now live in. One was the seed which grew into the Tree. The last was the egg which contained my great-great-grandfather. The thing they never talk about," she added with a rueful tilt to her head, her chin in her hand as she leant upon the table, "is how *long* it took for those things to grow. Pixies are incredibly lackadaisical about the passage of time."

My thoughts combined and I had a hard time controlling them; I'm afraid I blurted them out, one after another, with no context or consideration for my lady. The first was something to the effect of how beautiful she was—for that was the primary thought on my mind, that perhaps the magic of the wish explained her exquisite being. The second was, of course, that the fairies always told me I was born of a curse.

Naturally my lady, modest and clear-sighted as she is, focused on the latter of the two thoughts.

It had always been my intention to tell her eventually. Naturally I didn't like to bring it up out of turn, but I knew that if I was to properly serve my lady, she ought to know all the important things about me. I always knew that. But I had given the matter so little thought . . .

I tried to explain this, but I doubt any of it made sense. Fortunately, my lady was extremely kind.

"Come and sit back down," she said, and I obeyed. "Start at the beginning, and tell me everything together, like it's a story."

I suspect, in retrospect, that she often directs the pixies this way.

But I will admit I found it extremely helpful. In fact I will write it down now, because there is something about it—containing the entire story in one telling, or one page—rather than letting it contain me—which is revelatory.

This is what I told her:

"Much of this happened centuries upon centuries ago—for you must understand, I am very old, as most fairies are. My father was of the Grendale water fairy clan, and my mother was a trickster deity—that ancient kind of divine figure which can sometimes be helpful, and sometimes betray. The union was considered not only regrettable, but punishable by death at the time.

"However, some of the fairies in the clan's court felt that such a punishment was barbaric and ill-advised. For you see, my father was adept in magical arts, and some feared he might work some kind of revenge. But in the end nothing he did came to any good. He was killed, and the clan was in upheaval, and my mother could never be found. By that time, I had just barely turned one year old.

"The fairies stopped short of killing me. On a whim, the clan's cook took me in, saying they fancied a changeling for the work in the kitchens.

"Of course, I was not exactly a changeling. I was half fairy and half deity—neither one thing nor another. Often the fairies' matriarch would say they ought to have killed me, simply because there was no place for me to fit. But I think that, because of my mother's divine blood in me, none of the fairies were sure *how* I could be killed. I can be injured, of course, but otherwise proved to be just as long-lived as they were. I worked hard to serve the cook, and in time won their favor;

and because of that, it was decided I should serve in other ways, and so I became a knight.

"But there were always the older fairies who said I was a curse. It is very rare to have fairy children, you see; only the leaders of the clan may do so. But my father had been put to death because of my birth, and the clan suffered for his loss. Much of that suffering was attributed to me. Perhaps this makes little sense from the outside, but I was the only strange one in court, and had no voice to use against them; I knew nothing else.

"The cook celebrated the day I passed from squire to knight, and helped me summon Nessie for the very first time. Shortly after, they were accused of betraying the fairies' trust, and like my father, they were put to death. I have always considered myself responsible for that death. It is the trickster heritage in me; it is something that can not be escaped, like a terrible stroke of bad fortune that aims for those closest to me.

"Nessie and I wandered a good deal after that. It was in those days that we met Lancelot—and it was in those early, unguarded days that I confessed my past to him, something I never should have done. He only ever held it over my head. In the end, something—some sense of doom, or inevitability—drew me back to the fairy clan. By that time, years had passed, and opinions had turned. I was useful to them then in a way I hadn't been before. I knew of the outside world, and it felt natural to me to act as liaison. Additionally, I was adept as a knight and potion-maker. I became favored once more by the ruling family . . . and then, as you know, came Snow."

I had tried to do exactly as she said, tie everything together into one story. It was the first time I had ever attempted to do so. I'm not sure what about it surprised me: whether it was the string of deaths, or the shortness of the tale, or the fact that

155

I'd forgotten it enough to think I might be happy with Daisy. I finished and the fire still burned merrily before us, and the night still was young.

My lady's hand on my cheek brought my focus back into the room. I would have gladly kissed her, and thereby banished all thoughts of my past from my mind; but—perhaps because she knew this—she merely pressed her lips to my forehead and whispered in my ear, "Thank you."

"It was only right I tell you, my lady," I managed, somewhat stiffly. "You have been so kind as to trust me. And it is only fair you be on your guard."

She tilted her head as she considered me, and finally asked, "Would you like to know what I think?"

When I affirmed that I would, she leaned in once more and said, "Gold-Tree wished for safety. Your father and the Grendales were cursed because they could not provide safety for their own. *They* were cursed—not you. *They* carried out their sentences, again and again. You merely lived. *None of it was your fault.*"

Her words penetrated me very deeply, and there was nothing I could say. Seeing this, my lady rose and busied herself with something—making hot chocolate over the fire. I watched her all the while, silent, pondering. It wasn't until she returned to the bench and handed me a mug that I finally found my voice.

"It has taken me years to even consider the possibility which you see so quickly," I told her. "This—my quest for the Tree—Lancelot thought I undertook it in order to raise the cook, or even my father, or perhaps even to bring it to the Grendales themselves, in a sort of bid for reinstatement. But that was never why I sought the Tree. I sought it because . . . because I wanted to know . . . that I am alive. And that I am . .

. worthy of being so."

"You thought somehow the Tree would pass judgment on you?" my lady smiled. "It won't do that. But it *was* willing to heal you."

"Yes," I said softly. "And I am grateful. However . . . if you'll permit me . . . since meeting you, I have found that the question doesn't bother me the way it did before."

"Good," said she, caressing my cheek with a chocolatey kiss. "Because I don't see how it is a question at all."

My lady sleeps now, her head on my shoulder as I write. At last, the fire has died, and I am only barely able to see the page. Perhaps it is time I rested also.

Thirty-One

Conditions

~⚜~

Sir Rowan
  30th Day of the 1st Moon

Last night I carried my lady to her bed and settled her there before laying myself down near the hearth. I only mention it because this morning she came out of her room with at first a startled look, her eyes wide and her locket swinging on its chain, and then an amused glance as she saw me preparing tea.

"I worried you'd gone, especially after everything you were saying last night," she said without preamble as she filled her watering can. "Did you sleep out here? It was strange to wake without you nearby."

I paused to consider this, despite the fact that the tea kettle was whistling and needed to be tended to. "I did not mean to unnerve you, but I thought you would be more comfortable in your room."

"And wouldn't you have been, also?" My lady turned against the sink and looked me right in the eyes. A smile tugged at the corner of her mouth.

I sputtered, and finally managed, "My lady, it would have been unconscionably presumptuous of me."

"Hmm," she said, tossing her wild hair before focusing on her plants. "If you won't be presumptuous, I suppose *I* must be forward."

Well!

"My lady," I said, and though I tried very sternly to control myself, I'm not sure I succeeded; "what the both of us ought to be is tactical."

"About the ice dragon, I suppose you mean?" she smiled at me over her shoulder. "You're right. May I borrow a page from your journal while you cook?"

When she had finished watering her indoor garden, she took the page I offered her and sat at the table with it and my pen. As I stirred oatmeal, she began to write—and, fortunately, to narrate.

"The ice dragon isn't going to do anything, so it's up to us to make a plan. What I think we should do," she said, "is start by knowing what we *don't* want to happen. That way we're both on the same page, so to speak."

I nodded along, wondering if she was using the approach because of my mistake with the Tree's bark. But her first suggestion was entirely practical.

"First: we can't allow the ice dragon to simply fly away," said my lady as she wrote the first item in her list. "I really don't think he's that mobile, but this would be the worst case scenario. The last thing we want is for him to go down to town or start looking for the pixies."

"So whatever we do, we must be certain that our plan pens him in," I said, understanding her method. By imposing constraints on our plan, she actually made it easier to come up with viable ideas. "Or that he agrees to your escort, perhaps?"

"Yes. And the second thing: we shouldn't just kill him outright. We should give him another chance to talk."

"He seemed very unwilling to do so yesterday," I pointed out. Thinking of his cruelty to my lady, I added a little extra sugar into the oats.

"I know. But his tune might change once we've subdued him, or forced ourselves past his blockade, or whatever it is that we do," she said as she wrote.

"If it doesn't, we will not humor him," I said. "I suggest we avoid any circumstance in which he is allowed to talk at length."

My lady paused, but then I heard the scratch of the pen as she wrote this down too. "I didn't think of that, but I see your point. Given yesterday, he'll probably just . . ."

"Try to come between us," I suggested, "or make you doubt yourself."

"True. I have one last requirement," she said, and the tone of her voice warned me I might not like it. "If we *do* have to kill him, let me be the one to do it."

I set down my spoon and turned around. "Why, my lady?"

"It's not that I think you couldn't," she assured me. "He's always had an unfair advantage on you before. What I'm worried about is—word is going to get out about this. That's the whole reason Lavender sent us both, right? And—if the story is about a *knight* slaying a dragon, it might cause uproar. Or retaliation. But if the story is about me killing another dragon, then everyone—all the other dragons, I mean—they'll understand that the ice dragon probably got too close to the Tree."

Given my observations of Lavender, I think she sent us *both* on this trip just to meddle. Not that I'm not grateful. But she's not a woman who believes in overkill, as it were.

But I didn't bring that up. Instead, I asked, "What if the story is about you and a knight killing the dragon?"

My lady hesitated. "I think—well, they *could* be mad, like the ice dragon was, but I doubt they'll care too much, since the ice dragon is definitely in *my* territory. My family is known for being . . . eccentric. Honestly it's more likely that they won't even pay attention to that part of the story, though. They'll think people made it up to make knights seem useful," she explained to me with a small, apologetic smile.

It was interesting to hear her talk about her territory. There is a truth in what she says: after all, in most areas where a dragon is known to reside, the nearby town exists or perishes at the local dragon's whim. She is smaller than the ice dragon, true, but she is still one of the most impressive dragons I have seen—and on top of that she is smart enough to be a truly dangerous foe. I would much rather cross ten ice dragons than Daisy. I had wondered, up til that point, if she realized how much power she might have; it seemed that she did.

"In that case, my lady," I said, "it seems it is time for us to devise a plan."

"Yes. Something that doesn't involve letting him escape, killing him prematurely, or letting him ramble," she said as I doled out portions of breakfast.

"You're certain you don't want to simply collapse the cave around him, my lady?" I asked. Primarily I meant to tease her, but I can't deny I'd have liked that option, myself.

"No. On top of everything else, that'd create far too much disturbance in the forest," she informed me with a laugh.

"It sounds to me like you have another requirement in mind."

"Not disturbing the forest is always an assumed requirement," she retorted, smiling at me as I sat across from her. Our bowls steamed before us.

As we ate, we went over many possibilities. We quickly decided that the best way into the cave would be to first melt the ice with fire. "But you'll have to build the fire," she informed me, and with a becoming blush explained, "I know to you I seem very warm all the time, but I don't actually breathe fire."

"Do you have some other natural attack, my lady?" I asked, knowing that many dragons of different types *do* have different defenses. It occurred to me that knowing about hers would be very useful in planning.

She nodded. "Paralysis poison. It's a breath attack, like the fire. On smaller creatures, it lasts long enough that I can pick them up and move them. I don't think it would be effective for very long on the ice dragon, though. In the past I've done other things, too, like mesmerizing or confusing rabid creatures, but that was usually with the pixies' charms to help."

"Would the effect be strong enough to interrupt him if he attempts to blast us with ice?" I asked.

"Probably, especially because he'd have to draw a breath in first," she said thoughtfully. "I'd have to be quick."

"Perhaps while I tend the fire, you can be watching for the right moment," I suggested. "Even if he succeeds once or twice in rebuilding some of the ice, he can't continue to ice himself all the way back into the cave."

"I see what you're saying. You'll have to mind the water coming off the melted ice, though," she replied. "I think I can help divert that. I can keep it from raining on to the fire directly with my wings. Don't worry," she smiled, seeing the very beginning of my frown, "a fire has to be *very* hot before it has any effect on me."

I didn't realize I was so easy to read.

"Very well. So, we will have made our way into the cave, and temporarily incapciatated the dragon," I said with an effort. "Then what?"

My lady pursed her lips. "We'll ask again to talk, of course, but as you pointed out earlier, that probably won't hold his attention."

"Perhaps instead we should start more strongly," I said, "by informing him that the local townsfolk have demanded he leave."

"I don't think Lavender speaks for all the townsfolk," my lady said, "but I suppose that's close enough. Are you sure there isn't some way we can banish him directly back to wherever he came from?"

"I'm sure there is, my lady, but I'm not sure what we could do by ourselves," I answered truthfully.

Her eyes wandered the room as she considered this. At last she smiled. "What if we put him to sleep?"

"To sleep, my lady?"

"With herbs. By burning them in the fire! We'd have to protect ourselves, of course, and use a lot of my strongest plants, but then afterward we could splint his wing for him, as a sign of good faith, and perhaps bring in someone who can do the right magic."

"In essence, you want to *catch* the dragon," I summarized with a wary glance. "Exactly what did you do to him the first time, that you think he is weakened enough to make this possible?"

My lady became abashed and shrugged. "I may have up-rooted a nearby tree and swung it into his wing. Through the joint in his wing, actually."

"You did *what?*"

"And then I hit him in the head with the other end of it. The tree, I mean. At least, I'm pretty sure that's what I did. Come to think of it, he probably has some cracked teeth . . ."

I was aghast. "What about not disturbing the forest?"

"I didn't have time to think it over," she protested. "He'd frozen Nessie solid!"

She focused on scraping the remnants of oatmeal from her bowl, and did not meet my gaze. (She did say earlier that she liked how sweet it was.) I had the distinct impression that it wasn't for Nessie's sake alone that she had acted.

"Well," I said at last, "I must confess, I'm a bit impressed with our foe. The fact that he walked away from that at all is commendable."

My lady blushed bright crimson, no doubt picking up the light tone in my voice. When she looked up and saw me smile, she smiled back. "Everyone knows I take my job seriously," she said. "After he made a comment about wanting magic, *and* attacked you, it shouldn't have come as any surprise."

I took it that she meant "every dragon," and had a passing curiosity into this network of gossip and reputation. How did such solitary creatures learn of each other? I suppose they pick up little bits of news over time, and repeat them endlessly—much like any long-lived being.

"This is useful," I told her, and I could see she was a little surprised. I explained, "No doubt a part of the bravado we dealt with yesterday was born of fear. And if he is afraid of you . . ."

"Then it may be easier than we think to trick him," my lady concluded. "So, you're on board with my idea?"

"Completely," I assured her. And with that, we set about our preparations.

Thirty-Two

Confrontation

Daisy

Oh, the ice dragon day! Where do I even start?

Well, the first thing we had to do was make a fire, of course. I don't have much experience with fires at all, except at the keep. Even then, half the time it's the guests who do the fire maintenance. So right from the beginning, I was very glad to have Rhys along to point out things like how we'd have to bring lots of wood with us and maybe some fire-starting supplies, too.

When I realized how much wood we'd need, I figured we better go check on the ice dragon before actually setting the fire. It wouldn't do, I thought, to show up at his cave with a huge armload of wood and find that the place was open already. So Rhys and I flew over to check—and sure enough, the place was still closed up, and the ice dragon still refused to talk, even after I told him what would happen if he stayed in there. I know he heard me, too, because I could hear him rumbling.

I never would have realized that he was probably rumbling out of fear, had not Rhys pointed it out.

And I did feel a little bad for him—for the ice dragon, I mean. But when I mentioned this to Rhys, he said he didn't at all, because the ice dragon had started this confrontation, and kept it going. I suppose it's hard to feel sorry for someone who's knocked you unconscious and frozen your horse. And truthfully, Rhys was right. The ice dragon had had every opportunity to rise above his fears and his prejudices.

So, after that, we really got to work. It was nice working with Rhys, very efficient, but even so it took a little while—especially because I kept pausing to check the pixies. The sun was directly overhead by the time Rhys and I showed up at the cave again, our arms full of firewood from the keep. Rhys set about arranging the wood as I collected and broke down some of the downed trees nearby.

And really, once we got going, it was like clockwork. Exactly like we'd planned—which to me was a miracle! It's impossible to plan anything with pixies.

Rhys stood to one side of the cave entrance, all fitted up with gloves and his armor, a cloth tied carefully around his nose and mouth. He fed the fire and kept it burning. I stood to the other side, trying to control the melting ice. When it got thin in places I could break it, and by gouging channels in the dirt I could direct the flow of water away from Rhys and his fire. I even found that I could use my breath to blow away showers of droplets, creating an icy rain which more often than not fell all over Rhys and made him look like he was sparkling.

The problem was that the ice dragon didn't come forward, like we'd expected. We'd thought that he'd be right on the other side of the ice wall, trying to fortify it or stop us from melting it somehow. Instead, he cowered in the back of the cave. I could barely see him back there in the gloom.

On one hand, that made it pretty easy to get into the cave. Once the fire got going, the ice melted faster and faster. But on the other hand, this meant that all the bunches of sleepwort we'd brought weren't helpful. They were stacked in a pile behind Rhys, to be added to the fire as soon as the ice dragon was near enough to inhale the smoke. But he never came close enough.

Trusting Rhys to back me up despite the change in plan, I broke through the ice wall as soon as I could.

"You can't hide from us any longer," I called to the ice dragon.

"'Us,'" the dragon rumbled back, mocking me. "You're disgusting."

"The townspeople have requested that you leave," I said firmly. "And so do I. The Circle of Dragons knows this mountain is mine."

"You aren't a dragon," he snarled back.

Behind me, I heard Rhys scuffling as he put out the fire. I was glad he was too busy to be part of this conversation. "I am dragon enough to have been the one to send you cowering into this cave," I reminded the ice dragon.

"You'll drag me out when I'm dead," he insisted.

"I haven't expressed any desire to kill you. In fact, I'm offering to send you home. Peaceably."

"This is my home now. You should have thought it through before you summoned me!"

"I wasn't the one to summon you, as you know very—"

"You're one of *them* now. All knights are exactly the same."

Now, I respect Rhys very much, and I admire his knowledge and his self-reliance. And in the end, I didn't mind Sir Perceval very much. But the fact remains that it is a *terrible* insult to call a dragon a knight. It's like when the pixies call each other pinkie-swear breakers.

And I was so *frustrated* by him insisting all knights are the same. Because I had thought so too once, but then I had learned better. And it seemed obvious, even fundamentally necessary, to me now.

I roared—whether as a warning to him or to Rhys, or just to let go of my own anger, I'm not sure. Then I rushed him.

Looking back, of course I realize that this is what he wanted all along. I probably should have known it at the time—no doubt Rhys did—but I really haven't been in that many fights. Aside from play fights with my brother. Before Rhys showed up, most of our problems were just rabid bears or the occasional band of thieves.

The ice dragon reared up with a boulder in his claws. With a thunderous roar of his own, he threw it straight for me at point-blank range. I might have dodged it, but I worried in the last second that it would hit Rhys. So I took the blow to the chest.

It didn't stop me moving, though. I sat back and launched upward, flying awkwardly in the narrow cave. I had just enough space to get above the ice dragon. He breathed ice at me, but his control wasn't good. Probably his jaw was still hurting him. I dodged the ice and whipped his mouth closed with my tail. The last thing I wanted was for him to freeze Rhys.

A flash from the back of the cave told me that Rhys had

followed me in, unnoticed by the ice dragon. The cave still echoed from the roars, covering the noise of Rhys in his armor. I feinted at the ice dragon, making him rise up to swipe at me with his claws. My intention was to knock his head into the rock wall, to make him unconscious so that we could tie him up. I shifted so that I could hit him with my tail again, but as I rose the cave wall scraped at my left wing, making me falter. In that moment the ice dragon grabbed my back leg and pulled me down onto the ground.

I landed on my back. The worst possible position to be in. I got ready to breathe poison at him, thinking that he'd either swipe for my belly or try to ice me in place. I aimed very carefully for the pointy fangs that marked his open mouth. But just as I breathed in, in that little space where I held my breath before blowing it out again, the ice dragon's head jerked and fell away.

I scrambled up at once. Rhys had killed the ice dragon by cutting off its head.

Thirty-Three

Dead and Angry

Sir Rowan
   30th Day of the 1st Moon, cont.

The encounter with the ice dragon went exactly as to be expected. Daisy performed her part beautifully—if a little recklessly at the end. The moment she charged into the cave, I knew all bets had to be off.

And this is where my journal takes on the feeling of a necessary defense.

I know how important Daisy's rules are to her, of course. And I know how much she values life—though perhaps I see that better *now*, writing the evening after the entire affair, than I did at that particular moment.

I almost would rather not write about it. But, it is necessary to understanding what happened afterward.

The only moment I remember clearly is Daisy on the ground beneath the ice dragon. I had an opportunity and I did exactly what needed to be done. Now, yes, I suppose I could have knocked it out somehow, but that would have required extra thought and time that I did not have. A sword charmed by the fae to be as sharp and hard as diamond is not suited for knocking dragons out, in any case. I killed him before he could kill my lady.

The resulting mess was extremely cold and plentiful. My lady and I scrambled all the way out of the cave to get away from the scene. In the clearing, the snow wiped the traces of blood away from her white scales as she paced, agitated.

"He's dead," she kept repeating. "Didn't we agree *not* to kill him impetuously?"

"Forgive me, my lady," I said, and I must admit I said it icily, "but I considered his death preferable to yours!"

"How did you even do it? How did you cut through his scales? No, never mind, don't tell me. What we have to do is tell Lavender. But—"

My lady paused, perhaps noticing that the winter sun was already setting.

Seeing as the whole point of this endeavor had been to bring Daisy and I together, and to reinstate her position with Mme Lavender, I didn't like the idea of returning to town while she was so upset.

"She'll be in the middle of the dinner rush," I said, "and everyone in town will be there. It would be easier to go tomorrow mor—"

My lady turned back to me, eyes blazing. "Don't think I don't know what you're doing. You don't want me to make a report while I'm angry at you for going against the plan!"

"I'd prefer not to fight in front of the entire village," I returned.

"Fine," my lady growled. "Then we'll go back to the keep and fight, and come back tomorrow to clean up this mess."

I had half expected that she might make me *walk* up the mountain to the keep. Instead she carried me quite civilly, though it seemed to me I could feel the tension beneath her hide. The flight back to the keep might have given me a chance to reconsider, and to be calm—surely I *wanted* to be calm—but truthfully the idea that she was so tense, that she truly had *no* idea why I had acted, only made me more upset. By the time I made my way to the keep's kitchen, not even tea could render me calm.

My lady came barreling out of her room as soon as she'd changed, her hair wildly framing her face as she glared at me in the fire-lit room.

"What is the point of making plans with you if you are just going to break them?" she asked.

"What is the point of carrying through a plan if it means you get injured, or worse?" I retorted.

"I expected to get hurt. I *was* already hurt. It doesn't matter."

I could feel the heat rise in my face at the thought. "It does to me!"

"But we had a duty to see things through," she protested, not understanding.

"What good is that without *you*?" I repeated. "I would expect staying alive to be our primary duty!"

And, yes, I knew even as I said it how strange it was, that I should be arguing that, when only days ago I might have meekly given up if it was required of me. But I couldn't help it: that was what I felt. This was my new life, and I would not lose it.

"Then you should have made it one of your conditions at the beginning," Daisy told me. She was close enough to poke me in the chest.

"I thought it would be assumed!"

"Why? Why would we assume that when we both know we're going into a fight?"

"Because—because—" I couldn't explain this, not properly, and so instead I said, "You shouldn't act so recklessly regarding your own health when there are so many who rely on you."

"*I'm* the reckless one? *You're* the one who's now going to have all sorts of dragons seeking him out for revenge!" she shot back. This time she really did lay her hands on me, pressing into my shoulders as though to drive home her point. On her tiptoes, her eyes were level with mine. And her mouth was level with mine, too.

"I don't care about the other dragons," I insisted. "I only care about *you*."

"Well, then you should worry about how I'm supposed to keep you safe and enjoy your company when I'm having to fight off other dragons who want your blood all the time," she insisted. Her fingertips dug into my tunic, twisting the fabric.

"*I* will fight them," I said. It was only when I felt her body jerk at this that I realized I, too, was clinging tight to her waist.

"You will not," she growled, her eyes dark.

"*You* won't either," I insisted. "Not alone."

"You are trouble," she retorted. And then she kissed me. She kissed me harder than ever before, her body locked around mine, her hands tugging at my hair.

But I was torn. "Why don't you see how much you mean to me?" I asked, my words muffled by her embrace.

"Because you hide things," she returned promptly, her forehead against mine, her breath hot across my cheek. "Behind politeness, behind talk about duty. I know I have been conflicted too, but at least I know one thing—you don't need an excuse for how you feel."

"My lady," I murmured softly. "I am not conflicted. I know exactly how I feel. But I wasn't sure—"

"Be sure," she said. Her voice mellowed, and her kisses lingered between her words. "Show me, now."

I didn't need her to tell me twice. At once, I found her mouth, drawing her into my kiss as I turned us both, pressing her back into the wall.

Though I hated very much to have been at odds with her, the end result was perfectly right.

Thirty-Four

Close to You

Daisy

Well, the pixies do love a contradiction. My mother says her uncle always said it best. "There is no creature as contrary as a pixie," he'd say. And, "a pixie loves nothing more than a trick."

Sometimes I wonder if Fate itself is a pixie.

I *did* get very mad, and I must admit it was because I didn't think at all of myself. But Rhys was right: what good is duty if you're dead? I think what I learned from the whole affair, more than anything, is that duty only really works if it's paired with love. And even though I hadn't told him out loud quite yet, I think that ever since the moment Rhys had promised he'd look after the pixies with me, I'd loved him without reservation. Not because of the pixies exactly, but because of how willing he was to be kind.

And at last, with the ice dragon ordeal over, everything became rosy. The next day we went down and cleaned things up at the cave. I did the rites for the ice dragon—even though he hadn't been anything but mean, I thought he still deserved some respect. Rhys collected a claw and scale to show Lavender as proof.

"I don't really think she'll doubt us," I said.

"Perhaps not, my lady," he smiled back, "but it is best to be careful, is it not?"

I only rolled my eyes at him and smiled, because I knew he was teasing.

We caught Lavender just after lunchtime. She was pretty pleased with the result, I think. She hardly hesitated at all before saying that she'd repair the keep and let me stay on as caretaker. I realized then that perhaps Rhys had been right—maybe she *was* just trying to get us together.

Well, it worked.

Rhys and I sat on a bench in Market Square. I was still in my human form from when we talked to Lavender, and people waved as they passed. Some stood in corners and gossiped, but they didn't seem afraid. It seemed like good news was traveling fast.

When I mentioned this to Rhys, he agreed. He broke off half of the muffin Lavender had given us, along with steaming cups of tea. After giving me my portion, he said, "Of course, you were right last night, my lady. It isn't all good news, is it?"

"So you admit it." I grinned. "Yes—you're definitely going to need someone to look after you, at least for a little while. In case more dragons come looking."

"And you," he returned, very seriously. "You may find it convenient to have someone in town keeping an eye out for adventurous souls looking for the Tree of Life."

"I might." I eyed him over my drink. "Was this your plan all along?"

"I never had any plan," he assured me, "except to be closer to you."

"Hmm . . . that sounds like a yes."

Thirty-Five

Fate

Rhys
  1st Day of the 2nd Moon

I find I have been remiss in keeping my journal. However, since I doubt very much I will forget the conclusion of Daisy's and my hunt of the ice dragon, I will let that oversight rest.

However, there is one particular scene I'd like to mention. After Daisy and I had cleared up matters with Lavender and Officer Thorn in Belville, my lady honored me by inviting me up to properly meet the pixies. She said it was only fitting, as our destinies were now all intertwined—though she did not know, when she said that, just how intertwined they were.

Only by walking in holding Daisy's hand was I able to perceive the pixies' hiding place. To me, it seemed that we were walking straight into a waterfall, and then straight into rock. But nonetheless I followed where Daisy led, and soon found myself in a familiar place—at the foot of a massive cave, looking up at a brilliant, illuminated Tree.

The primary difference, of course, was the pixies themselves. Knowing them as I do now, I have no idea how my lady kept them from swarming me when she first brought me to the cave, injured. Now that I could stand and fend for myself, the pixies flew all about me, tugging at my clothes and laughing in my ears.

Daisy, too, was laughing. "I'm sorry," I could hear her say, just barely, over the buzzing of so many dragonfly-like wings. "We don't often get visitors, as you know."

Her humor made me smile, which in turn made the pixies even more fascinated by my unfamiliar features. When the sea of pixies finally parted—taking with it more than a few strands of my hair and threads from my cloak—I found myself face to face with three more dignified personages. The Elders, my lady had called them. One fluttered on wings of gold, one hovered in shadow, and one pirouetted in the center, her entire body no bigger than my hand.

"Child of Our Bright Wren, the Trickster," she said to me, having introduced herself as Sha. I glanced at Daisy, startled to recognize one of my mother's titles. Trickster deities are often associated with animals—a fact it seemed Daisy did not know, for she looked surprised but completely unconcerned. The pixie, too, was unconcerned, although I had expected concern to be the natural result any time the title of a deity renowned for theft and trickery was spoken.

And yet instead . . . the little pixie, Sha, smiled at me. "Did you not know that *She* is the deity I serve?"

I think, had Daisy not been holding on to me, I might have fallen over.

Seeing this, the pixie laughed, and all around us the other pixies echoed her mirth.

Daisy, too, seemed to think this a cause of celebration. "I had never even thought to ask, Sha," she said, and added to me, "I suppose it does make sense—the pixies love to play pranks."

"But there is more," said Sha solemnly. "We do love tricks, yes, but there must be a rhyme to them. The rhyme to Her greatest trick is that we live. Do you understand this, Child of Hers?"

I had to admit that I did not.

"Long, long ago," said Sha, "when we were seeking refuge, Gold-tree said she could make the plants grow. Cold Breeze said they could hide our home. And I prayed to my deity to protect our lives. She brought us three great boon—one cave, one egg, and one a gift she freed from the clutches of greed, a treasure she found far away. A seed. From that seed came our Tree."

Daisy turned to me, confused. "So one of the gifts the pixies received was actually . . ."

". . . stolen from the Grendales at the same time I was conceived," I said slowly. "In order to answer the pixies' prayer for safety, my mother created mayhem elsewhere. Well, that is very much the trickster way of doing things."

"You see," said Sha, clapping her hands. "And now the cycle is completed with the final gift!"

"What is that?" I asked cautiously.

It wasn't simply Sha, but all three Elder pixies who spoke. "You. The closest link to Our Wren!"

A long time later, Daisy and I managed at last to slip away from the pixies' celebration. She took my hand and led me down into her quarters, where at last we were alone, and it was almost quiet. My head was still spinning. But when I looked at her, she smiled, and I could feel my confusion ease.

"I think it does kind of make sense," she said to me. "If you think about it—we do need you. A Tree, a Guardian—but also a Guide, of sorts. Someone to help us interact with the outside world. Do you—do you mind?"

"Of course not," I said at once. "I had already resolved to serve you. But it is strange to think . . ."

". . . that it might have been meant to be this way?" Daisy tilted her head. "I suppose it *is* odd. But what's done is done, and I have a feeling it was done for a reason. Don't you think that's the only thing about all this nonsense that makes *sense*? After all, neither of us would be here without the theft of the Tree, and now that we've found each other, we can keep it safe."

At that, I took both her hands in mine. "And you are glad to have found me?" I asked, just to be sure.

"Of course I am," she said, smiling. "You know that."

"But I'll admit I am trouble—even more so, perhaps, because of my parentage. Will you let me stay and aid you, anyway?"

"That," said Daisy, smiling slyly, "depends on your reason."

I did not hesitate. "My lady, my reason is that I love you."

"Oh! Well in that case, it's alright," she said, bringing me in to her embrace. "In fact, it's perfect. Because I love you, too."

Afterword

. . . once upon a time, a knight fell in love with a dragon, and a queen reigned without a king. And they lived in the shadow of a great tree which reached to the heavens, and they were very happy.

Even if they were plagued by pixies.

And other knights.

And dragons.

But really, what's a happily ever after without a little bit of a challenge in it?

About the Author

Elle adores cozy mysteries, fairy tales, and above all, learning new things. As a historian and educator, she believes in the value of stories as a mirror for complicated realities. She currently lives in New Jersey with a grumpy tortoise and a three-legged cat.

Find more stories of Red and her friends at ellehartford.com. And while you're there, sign up for Elle's newsletter to get bonus material including short stories and extra epilogues!

Also by Elle Hartford

If you haven't already, don't forget to check out *Cold as Snow*, where Sir Rowan got his start in Belville! And check out Daisy and Sir Rowan's future in *Strong in Love*, the second Pomegranate Cafe Romance novella.

Cold as Snow
In this magical twist on a familiar tale, alchemist Red sets out to answer the riddle behind deadly apples and a cursed mirror . . . *Who gets to decide who's fairest of all? And who would be willing to kill over it?* She'll need all her old friends—and eight new ones, too!—to put this case on ice.

https://books2read.com/AlchemicalTales2/